THE BRONC RIDER'S BABY

BY
JUDY DUARTE

First Published in Great Britain 2017
By Mills & Boon, an imprint of HarperCollins*Publishers*
1 London Bridge Street, London, SE1 9GF

ISBN: 978-0-263-92300-1

23-0517

Ou ... ble
pr ... gging and
ma ... ations of
the

Pri
by

"I wasn't expecting you so soon."

Nate glanced at the baby, then touched a little foot that peeked out from her blanket. The flicker of a smile crossed his face.

As if sensing that Anna was watching him, he straightened and caught her eye. They gazed at each other for a beat, long enough for her to realize a little dust and perspiration did very little to lessen his sexy appeal. In fact, it made him even more manly, more…

Oh, wow. It seemed to be getting awfully warm in here.

"Do you want to stay with the baby?" he asked. "Or would you rather go outside and talk to me?"

"Let's take a walk," she said, liking the sound of it.

Nate nodded, then swung out his arm in a gallant "after you" manner.

Anna started toward the door, but when she walked past the handsome cowboy and caught a whiff of an alluring scent of leather and musk, she wasn't so sure being alone with him was such a good idea after all.

* * *

Rocking Chair Rodeo:

Cowboys—and true love—never go out of style!

Since 2002, *USA TODAY* bestselling author **Judy Duarte** has written over forty books for Mills & Boon Cherish, earned two RITA® Award nominations, won two Maggie Awards and received a National Readers' Choice Award. When she's not cooped up in her writing cave, she enjoys traveling with her husband and spending quality time with her grandchildren. You can learn more about Judy and her books at her website, www.judyduarte.com, or at Facebook.com/judyduartenovelist.

To Gail Duarte, my "twin" sister-in-law,
who took me to the World's Oldest Rodeo.
And yes, it actually *was* my first rodeo!

Chapter One

Nate Gallagher had run with the bulls in Pamplona and ridden some of the toughest broncs in rodeos all over the country, but he'd never faced anything as scary and as unnerving as this.

What in the hell was he going to do with a premature baby girl? He'd bet he had champion belt buckles at home that weighed as much or more than she did.

The neonatal nurse, who'd just finished strapping little Jessica into her carrier, pointed to a white plastic bag bearing the hospital logo. "I've packed some bottles and formula for you to take home. Are you ready to go?"

Hell no. His heart was pounding so hard he thought it might break out of his chest, and he was sweating like crazy. But he'd be damned if he'd show any sign of fear.

"Yep." He reached for the baby carrier that would fit into the car seat base he'd secured in the backseat of his pickup, amazed that it felt just as light now as it had when he'd brought it into the Brighton Valley Medical Center. If he hadn't glanced inside where baby Jessica was dozing, he'd never know she was there. But she *was* there—and leaving the safety of the hospital to go with him.

Oh, man, this was happening way too fast. It had taken every bit of his courage to sign her release forms moments ago. Sure, she'd gained a pound or two since her birth. But why couldn't they have kept her a little longer, until she'd grown bigger—like the size of a kid entering kindergarten?

If they had, he'd feel a lot better about dealing with her. At least she'd be able to talk and tell him if he was doing something wrong.

"Mr. Gallagher?" a soft, feminine voice said from behind him.

As he turned, he caught sight of a petite blonde in his peripheral vision. He might consider the attractive woman worth his full masculine attention if he'd met her in a bar, throwing back a shot of tequila with her friends. But here in a hospital, holding a patient file in her hands? All bets were off.

"Yes," he said.

"I'm Anna Reynolds."

Was he supposed to know her?

She must have sensed his confusion because she added, "I'm the social worker assigned to your case."

Just the words *social worker* and *case* were an unsettling reminder of the years he'd spent in foster care and enough to stop him dead in his tracks. The only reason he'd stepped up and claimed paternity was to keep the tiny girl out of the system.

The woman—Anna, Ms. Reynolds or whatever he was supposed to call her—offered him a warm smile, no doubt meant to disarm him. "It's standard procedure."

For whom? The hospital? Or for the state of Texas?

He clutched the plastic handle and pulled the carrier close to his side, as if he could prevent anyone from taking the newborn away from him, his grip as tight as his gloved hand once held the braided leather rein on the back of a bronc charging out of a bucking chute.

"I'll be stopping by your house regularly for a while," she said.

Again with the smile. He had to admit it was a nice one. A pretty one. Under any other circumstances, he would look forward to having regular visits from the attractive blonde. But not when he knew she'd be checking up on him. Not when she had the power to remove little Jessica from his home.

And how weird was that? He was scared spitless to take custody of a child, a newborn, no less. Yet at the same time, he was hell-bent on keeping that baby safe.

And far, far away from Kenny Huddleston, the man responsible for her mother's death.

Following Kenny's brutal assault, Beth had gone into premature labor and later died of a brain bleed.

He wondered if the court had ordered the social worker's involvement. "Does this have anything to do with Beth?"

"No, it doesn't. Although I'm sorry for your loss."

Nate nodded, accepting the condolences, although he couldn't actually say he was grieving for Beth. Not that he didn't care. He did. But he was more saddened by the child's loss of her mother.

In truth, he really hadn't known Beth all that well. If he had, if they'd been closer, he might have been able to talk her out of going back to Kenny and marrying him. Or, at least, he might have convinced her to leave the guy before that fatal beating.

"The hospital sends me out to check on the families of preemies or seriously sick babies," the social worker added. "The parents usually have a lot of questions and concerns when they take their little ones home after a stay in the NICU."

She had that right. He'd be stressed and concerned even if Jessica had been born the size of a teenager. He glanced at the tiny girl, who didn't look a thing like him. But then again, she really didn't resemble Beth, either.

When he returned his gaze to Ms. Reynolds, he tried to manage a disarming smile of his own. "I won't be taking her home right away. We're going to stay on the ranch where I work. I'll have plenty of help there."

"That's good. I'm glad you'll have some support."

She opened the file she was holding and jotted down a note.

What had she written? Was it something about his judgment, his competency, his ability to parent?

If she weren't so pretty—and if she didn't have any power over him—he wouldn't even consider making an excuse to escape her attention.

"I understand that you were recently granted custody," she said.

It had taken a few days to get that ironed out, thanks to the help of an attorney, an overworked foster system and his friend's connections.

"The baby is mine," Nate said. "I'm her…father." At least that's what Beth had claimed.

Nate had his doubts, though. They'd only dated a short while. And the two times they'd had sex he'd used protection. If he had to guess, he'd say there was a far better chance that the child was Kenny's.

"Do we have the address of the place where you'll be staying?" Ms. Reynolds asked.

"Yep. You sure do. Are you familiar with the Rocking Chair Ranch?"

"I've heard about it. From what I understand, it's a home for retired cowboys."

Nate nodded his agreement.

"What's your connection with the place?" she asked.

Would she find him lacking if he admitted to being a ranch hand, to just being a cowboy? Maybe, but she was going to find out soon enough. "I'm employed there."

"What kind of work do you do at the retirement home?" she asked.

"The Rocking C is also a working cattle ranch." Nate glanced down at the sleeping infant in the carrier. "I guess it's going to be a nursery now, too."

Again the social worker smiled, reminding him of sunshine, warm breezes, spring flowers and all that was right in the world. But things were far from right. Even before this, his once-stellar career had been shot to hell.

And now he was going to be…a father.

"Are you a cowhand?"

He hoped she didn't have any objections to that line of work, although he couldn't rest on his laurels any longer, so he didn't tell her what he used to do, what he couldn't do any longer.

"My grandfather had a couple of friends who are living there, so they put in a good word for me. But don't worry. I can support a baby. I've also managed to sock some cash away."

At that she glanced up, her brow furrowed. "I'm not concerned about that. Of course, if you had any financial concerns, I could give you a few referrals to social services."

He'd rather die than rely on someone else's generosity ever again. "I won't need anything like that."

She smiled and gave a little shrug. "That's good to know, but I'm just a phone call away." She glanced down at her paperwork. "I assume we have your number."

"Yep." He nodded at the file in her hand. "It's all

there. But you might want to make a note that the cell phone reception on the Rocking C is almost nonexistent, so if you need to get a hold of me, you'd better call the ranch office."

"All right." Again she glanced down at the open file in her hands.

When she looked up, Nate noticed the unique color of her eyes. They were a honey brown. He supposed you'd call them hazel, with specks of gold and green.

But it doesn't matter what color the social worker's eyes are.

He returned his focus to the baby and a sudden need to escape what felt more like an inquisition than helpfulness. "Well, I hate to cut this short, but I have to get out of here. She eats every hour or two, so I want to get back to the ranch before she needs another bottle."

"Do you mind if I walk you out?" Ms. Reynolds asked.

Actually, he could use all the support he could get. And if she were anyone else, he'd let her catch a ride all the way to the ranch. But she wasn't someone who could help.

Still, even though he felt compelled to duck out of the hospital and leave her in his dust, he nodded his agreement, accepting what he couldn't change.

After they both removed the disposable covering the NICU visitors had to wear over their clothing, as well as the goofy-looking paper booties that went over their shoes, Nate and the attractive social worker exited, leaving the safety of the incubators and nursing staff behind.

As they walked along the corridor to the elevator, the soles of his boots created an interesting harmonic cadence with the click of her heels.

"It's a big day," she said. As if noticing the worry that was probably etched on his face, she glanced at the baby and added, "Taking home a newborn for the first time can be both exciting and a little unnerving."

He wouldn't say it was exciting, but it was certainly unsettling enough to make the toughest cowboy quake in his Tony Lamas. Rather than admit to any uneasiness, let alone a fear of failure, he didn't respond either way.

Thankfully, she let the subject drop as they rode the elevator down to the lobby. Once they'd walked out the double glass doors and stepped onto the hospital grounds, the sun was shining warm and bright. The birds chirped overhead, and the water fountain bubbled and gurgled as if it was a perfect Texas afternoon, but Nate knew better. He looked down at the sleeping infant. How could something so small cause so many uncertainties?

"Do you need any help getting that carrier into its base?" she asked.

"No, I've got it."

"Okay, then I'll let you go. I have a home visit to make."

So he wasn't her only... Her only what? Patient? Client? Case? Either way, that was a bit of a relief.

"Thanks for your concern," he told her. "I'm sure

we'll be just fine, Ms. Reynolds." He hoped his assurance worked, even though it was a line of bull.

She extended a manicured hand to him. "Please call me Anna."

His grip was gentle, but he couldn't help comparing the softness of her skin to his work-roughened calluses.

The afternoon sunlight danced upon the long, white-gold strands in her hair, tempting him to touch it, to watch it slip through his fingers and…

He shook off the inappropriate thought. Anna Reynolds was a beautiful woman, no doubt. In another world, in another life and time, he would have tried to wine and dine her, to date her and see where that might lead.

But even if they were now on a first-name basis, there was no way he'd think of the social worker assigned to his case in a romantic way.

Not when she had the power to take Jessica away from him and place the tiny, fragile baby in foster care.

Two days later, after leaving the Brighton Valley Medical Center, Anna made the forty-five-minute drive to the outskirts of Wexler, where the Rocking Chair Ranch was located. Her GPS told her she was getting close, but the actual driveway wasn't clear.

When she spotted a small mom-and-pop grocery store along the way, she stopped to purchase a bottle of water and a granola bar.

"How's it goin'?" the friendly clerk asked as she totaled the sale.

That was exactly what she planned to ask Nate when she arrived—without the Southern twang, of course. "Not bad." For a workday.

Anna pulled a twenty-dollar bill from her purse. "I'm heading to the Rocking Chair Ranch. Do you know where it is?"

"It's about a mile from here. Just look for a long line of mailboxes along the right side of the road. After that you'll see a yellow sign that points out the entrance. You can't miss it."

"Thanks." She took her purchases to the car. After opening the granola bar and taking a couple of bites, she continued the drive.

Sure enough, just ahead she spotted a string of mailboxes, most of them rusty or dented. Fifty yards farther, she saw the sign. Black cursive letters announced that she'd reached the Rocking Chair Ranch, a red arrow pointing the way.

She flipped on her blinker and turned onto a long, graveled road. Several horses grazed in a pasture that was enclosed by white fencing, the weathered rails in need of a fresh coat of paint.

Moments later she spotted a red barn, several corrals and a sprawling ranch house. In the shade of a big wraparound porch, several elderly men sat in wooden rockers flanked by clay pots filled with red-and-pink geraniums. It was a peaceful setting, and she could see why a retired cowboy or rancher would feel comfortable living here.

She wasn't exactly sure where to park her car, but decided upon a space next to a silver-gray pickup. Then she shut off the ignition, grabbed her purse and briefcase and made her way toward the house. As she strolled over the uneven path to the front porch, she was glad she'd chosen to wear flats today instead of heels.

Along the walkway, she passed an old tree stump that appeared to have been there for years. A patch of orange-and-yellow marigolds encircled it, making it a rather odd but nice lawn decoration. About ten feet away, in the center of the grass, sat a wooden cart filled with daisies.

As she bypassed a ramp that provided handicap access and approached wooden steps, the men in rocking chairs noted her arrival with a smile. When one tried to stand, she motioned for him to remain seated. The others seemed more interested in watching the activity in the nearest corral, where a cowboy worked with an Appaloosa gelding.

But it wasn't just any cowboy. It was Nate Gallagher.

Anna slowed to a stop and watched the man gentle the nervous horse with a skill that seemed inborn. His movements were a sight to behold. With those broad shoulders and narrow hips, his black Stetson angled just right, *he* was a sight.

He filled his boots, those worn jeans and a chambray shirt as if they'd been made with him in mind.

Back at the hospital, his handsome appeal had

been hard to ignore, but she'd noted a nervousness about him.

That certainly wasn't the case now. He was clearly in his element on the Rocking C, where he moved with both strength and grace, his self-confidence apparent.

As Anna continued to watch him work, glued to the way he spoke to the horse, an array of Western movies and their male stars flashed in her mind. Yet Nate stood out from all of them.

Because he was real, Anna decided. In fact, he was so authentic, she could easily imagine him walking down an Old West street, a leather holster slung low on his hips, two Colt 45s at the ready. She'd never been attracted to cowboys before, but there was something fascinating about this one, something sexy and alluring.

He glanced her way for a moment then returned his full attention to the gelding. He obviously knew what he was doing with the horse, but how was he doing with little Jessica?

For that reason, romantically speaking, Nate Gallagher was strictly off-limits.

"Can I help you?" a male voice asked from behind.

She glanced over her shoulder to see an elderly cowboy with a thick head of white hair and a warm glimmer in his eyes. She slowly spun around, switched her briefcase to her left hand and greeted him with the customary shake. "I'm Anna Reynolds, a social worker with the Brighton Valley Medical Center. I came by to visit Mr. Gallagher and the baby."

"Nice to meet you. I'm Sam Darnell, the Rocking C foreman. I'll let Nate know that you're here. In the meantime, why don't you go in the house? Joy, the ranch cook, has the baby. Last I knew, they were both in the kitchen."

"Thank you." Yet instead of going inside, as Sam had suggested, Anna said, "I imagine having a baby around is a bit of an adjustment for everyone. How are things going?"

"As good as can be expected, I suppose. Little Jessie isn't much bigger than a peanut, but Joy says she's taking to the bottle just fine. She's also going through the diapers, which I suspect is a good sign."

Anna smiled. "Yes, that's a very good sign." But there'd been more behind her question than that. She'd also wanted to know how Nate was doing. Was he adjusting to fatherhood? Was he bonding with his daughter?

In spite of the air of confidence he'd tried to project when he'd taken the baby home from the hospital, she'd sensed his discomfort and uneasiness. But she didn't blame him for that. Suddenly being responsible for a newborn could be daunting under the best of circumstances, but it was even more stressful and worrisome when the baby was premature.

She stole another peek at the handsome cowboy, her gaze lingering longer than it should.

"When you wanted to know how 'things' were going," the white-haired foreman said, "I guess you were actually wondering about how Nate was doing."

She returned her focus to Sam. Normally, she kept

her worries to herself, but she didn't think complete honesty would hurt in this situation. "From what I understand, he just learned about the baby's existence a couple of months ago. And since... Well, with the mother's death, he has to deal with this all alone."

"He's not alone," Sam said. "He's got everyone here to help out."

That was good. Wasn't it?

Still, she was pretty astute herself, and something seemed off. She just wasn't sure what it was. Maybe it was the fact that there were so many people here, including a bunch of old cowboys with who-knew-what kind of backgrounds.

Concern twisted into a bulky knot in her chest. No, something about this setup didn't feel right.

She hoped Nate was prepared for and even looking forward to being a father, but in spite of what he'd implied at the hospital, she hadn't been convinced. And she knew from experience what happened when a man didn't step up and take on a paternal role. Her own father certainly hadn't wanted to be a daddy. He might have tried to do the right thing and married Anna's mother when she'd gotten pregnant, but the couple had been young, and their marriage had been in trouble from the start. They'd fought from sunup to sundown, and eventually her dad had run off, abandoning his wife and child.

But this wasn't about Anna or the man who'd disappointed her. It was about human nature, and that's what had her worried.

She shook off the unpleasant memory and focused

on the case at hand. "I'd better go inside. I'd like to look in on the little 'peanut.'"

Sam didn't respond, but then why would he? She'd already started for the house before she'd completed her last sentence.

When she reached the porch, where the two oldsters sat, she offered them a casual "Hello" then opened the screen door and stepped inside. Before she could scan the living room, a long, appreciative whistle sounded from out on the porch.

"Now that's what I call a pretty little gal," one of the men said. "You think she's applying for a job here?"

The other chuckled. "It'd sure be nice if she was. I like living on a ranch, but you can't beat the pretty feminine scenery."

Anna probably ought to consider that a compliment, but that was another thing that made her uneasy. She didn't know anything about these men. Not that she expected them to be doddering old fools, completely oblivious to those around them. But was this really a good place to raise a baby?

She was just about to venture into the house, assuming she'd have to find the kitchen on her own, when she spotted a gray-haired man sitting in a brown vinyl recliner. He was holding a bottle and a small bundle wrapped in pink flannel.

So she approached the elderly resident and asked, "How's little Jessica doing today?"

He looked up and grinned, his tired eyes sparking with mirth. "She'd probably be a whole lot happier if

Joy was feeding her, instead of an old coot like me. But I'm getting the hang of this."

"I can see that." Anna offered him a smile of her own then introduced herself and told him why she'd come.

"You probably ought to talk to Joy or to one of the women," he said. "I'm just a temporary babysitter."

She'd like to talk to everyone here—the residents, the cook, the nurses. She'd especially like to talk to Nate. But apparently, until he was able to come inside to meet with her, the "temporary sitter" would have to do.

"How about her daddy?" Anna asked. "How's he adjusting to bottles and diapers?"

"Like most rodeo cowboys, I s'pose. He can handle a wild horse a hell of a lot better than he can a tiny baby." The old man may as well have waved a big red flag in front of the social worker.

"Is that a fact?" Anna had known that Nate worked on a ranch, but she hadn't realized he was also involved in the rodeo. But neither of those things had anything to do with him being a good father, one who was devoted to his daughter and eager to spend time with her. "I'm sure he'll get used to having a baby around before you know it."

The oldster chuckled. "I sure hope so. When he brought her home a couple of days back, he was as skittish as a colt in a thunderstorm. I'd be just as helpless. So it's a good thing he's got Joy and the nurses to help him day and night. 'Course Joy never had any kids of her own, but that don't matter. Women are just naturally maternal."

Anna suspected there were a lot of people in the old man's generation who believed that, but parenting wasn't just a woman's job. These days a lot of men quickly settled into their daddy roles and took an active interest in their newborns.

She just hoped that Nate wasn't skirting his emotional responsibility and letting everyone else take care of the baby. She'd really like him to step up and take part in his daughter's care.

"You want to feed her?" the gray-haired sitter asked. "I'm doing okay now, but I gotta tell you, when Joy handed her to me and asked me to feed her while she fixed our lunch, my heart started thumping and bumping like the pistons in a beat-up jalopy."

Anna's smile deepened. "You look like you're doing just fine, Mr....?"

"Mayberry," he said. "But call me Rex."

When the screen door squeaked open, Anna glanced over her shoulder to see who'd entered the house. The moment she spotted Nate, her heart skipped a couple of beats then sputtered back to life, thumping and bumping like those same pistons in Rex's jalopy.

Nate removed his battered Stetson, which had left a damp impression mark on his light brown hair, and held it in front of him. "Sam said you wanted to talk to me."

"Yes, I do. Is now a good time?"

"I guess so."

But not really? Most new parents were pleased

to know someone from the hospital had stopped to check on them, but she suspected he felt threatened by her arrival. And that sent up another red flag, one she'd have to keep in mind while she was here today and during her follow-up visits.

"Maybe I should have called first," she said.

He shrugged a single shoulder. "I just wasn't expecting you so soon."

He glanced at the baby then touched a little foot that peeked out from her blanket. The flicker of a smile crossed his face—a good sign, no?

As if sensing that Anna was watching him, he straightened and caught her eye. They gazed at each other for a beat, long enough for her to realize a little dust and perspiration did very little to lessen his sexy appeal. In fact, it made him even more manly, more…

Oh, wow. It seemed to be getting awfully warm in here.

"Do you want to stay with the baby?" he asked. "Or would you rather go outside and talk to me?"

She glanced at Rex, who was studying them as if they were actors on a stage. Maybe it would be best if they didn't have an audience.

"Let's take a walk," she said, liking the sound of it. She suspected Nate would feel better and be more relaxed outdoors. She certainly would.

"You got this, Rex?" Nate asked. "The baby's not too much for you? I can ask Joy to come out here and relieve you."

"Nope." The elderly man glanced down at the baby and smiled. "We're doin' just fine."

Nate nodded then swung out his arm in a gallant, "after you" manner.

Anna started toward the door, but when she walked past the handsome cowboy and caught a whiff of an alluring scent of leather and musk, she wasn't so sure being alone with him had been such a good idea after all.

Chapter Two

Nate followed Anna outside and onto the porch, where Gilbert Henry and Raul Santiago sat in their rockers. The creaks they were making as they swayed back and forth in their chairs slowed to a stop, their attention undoubtedly captured by the attractive social worker.

It was no secret around here that, back in the day, both of the retired cowboys had been ladies' men. Before the accident, Nate had been one, too. But not anymore. Even if he'd adapted to the life changes he'd been forced to make—the dashed dreams and altered career path—there was a five-pound two-ounce change that had turned him from a carefree bachelor to a man dead set on becoming a good father—or at least one that was adequate.

He just hoped that Ms. Reynolds—or rather Anna—realized how hard he was trying.

While he was determined to keep the attractive social worker in a professional light, it was a struggle. Every time he looked at her, he focused on her appearance. And now, as they stepped off the porch, he couldn't seem to keep his eyes off the gentle sway of her hips or the way that long blond hair swished and shimmered down her back.

He didn't need to glance at Gil or Raul to know what they were thinking. He sensed their interest and imagined they were sporting grins and winking at each other. He was also prepared for the ribbing he'd get, as well as the advice they'd offer him as soon as Anna left the ranch.

If she were any other beautiful woman, he wouldn't need any prodding or pushing. He'd never been shy. But Anna was different.

As she moved away from the shady porch and into the light of day, the platinum strands in her hair shimmered. Some women might pay good money to have highlights like that, but he'd bet a month's pay that Anna was a natural blonde.

He followed her to the lawn and waited while she placed her purse and briefcase on top of the old tree stump.

"Where to?" he asked.

"Nowhere in particular. I thought we should talk in private."

Nate doubted that she'd want a tour of the ranch, so he wasn't sure which direction to go, but definitely away from Gil and Raul. As he started toward the outbuildings, Anna fell into step beside him.

"Jessica looks good," she said.

Nate thought so, too, although he had no idea what signs might indicate she wasn't healthy or thriving. Rather than admit his lack of experience or reveal his incompetence, he said, "I'll sure be happy when she gains a few pounds."

"That shouldn't take very long. You'll be surprised at how quickly she'll grow."

It seemed as though it might take forever, but Anna was probably right. The same thing happened with a colt or a calf. The more they nursed, the bigger they got. It was just going to take a little while. Hopefully, he could spend that time here on the Rocking C, where he had plenty of help.

"She'll be toddling around before you know it," Anna added. "And then you'll have other things to worry about."

"Like *what*?" The minute he uttered the worry-laced question, he wanted to temper it somehow. He hadn't meant to reveal any insecurities he might have—and not just about infants, but fatherhood.

"For one thing," she said, "making sure the electrical sockets are protected from little fingers. And watching her closely so she doesn't climb up on something and fall. You'll also have to keep medications and cleaning supplies out of her reach."

Crap. There was so much he didn't know. "Maybe I'd better get some books on the subject."

"That will help, but during each stage of development, the pediatricians are pretty good at pointing out the things you should be concerned about in terms of health and safety."

"Thank God for that." The moment those words rolled off his tongue, he wished he could reel them back in before she realized how afraid he was that he'd slip up, that Jessie might be better off in someone else's care.

Anna's steps slowed, and as she turned to face him, she used her hand to block the sun from her eyes, which were almost a golden-brown hue today. "When's her first doctor's appointment?"

"Monday at four o'clock. They told me it's just to check her weight."

"Would you like me to meet you there?" she asked.

Hell, he'd love to have someone go with him—*anyone*. But did he really want that to be a social worker?

What if the baby hadn't gained any weight? What if Anna thought Jessie would be better off living with someone else?

Kenny might be locked up, but he had some sketchy family members, and maybe one of them would try to gain custody. From what Nate had heard, several of them had done time for various crimes such as assault, drunk and disorderly conduct or driving while under the influence.

"That's nice of you to offer," he said, "but it's not necessary."

When Anna didn't respond, he stole a peek at her, saw her forehead creased ever so slightly.

Hoping she didn't think he was skirting her, he added, "It's not that I don't want you to come. You can certainly meet me there if you want to."

"We'll see how my day goes," she said. "I'm usually off by four o'clock—unless something comes up."

They continued to walk along the lawn-flanked path to the corral where he'd been working with that new gelding a few minutes ago.

"So how are *you* doing?" Anna asked.

Him? He was nervous as hell and afraid he'd drop little Jessie or do something wrong. He also hadn't been able to sleep worth a damn because he kept waking up to check on her and make sure she was still breathing. But he didn't want to reveal any sign of weakness, so he chuckled and made light of it. "*Me?* I'm fine as frog's hair."

She laughed at his response. The lilt of her voice was enough to make him relax for the first time since she'd arrived. "Now, that's cute."

He hadn't meant to be cute. Was she a big-city girl laughing at his country ways? "It's just a saying I picked up from one of the retired cowboys who lives here."

She shifted slightly as if trying to avoid the sunlight from shining in her eyes. "Today, while I had lunch in the hospital cafeteria with a coworker, your name came up."

So much for relaxing around her. Why had his name come up? Had they been discussing him—and his case?

"One of the aides said you used to be a patient, that

you had a run-in with a wild horse. And one of the cowboys mentioned you were involved in the rodeo."

He'd been more than involved. He'd actually made a name for himself—until his injury. And until the doctor's diagnosis brought about a real reckoning on many levels. "I've still got friends who're on the circuit, but I gave it up."

"Why?"

Did it really matter? He shrugged a single shoulder. "I had more than a little 'run-in' with a bronc last year, and the doctors said I couldn't ride anymore. So I landed this job."

Her brow scrunched. "That sounds like a big change of pace."

It had been a *huge* change. And a real blow to his ego. Giving up the rodeo had been tough because, if he wasn't a star or a champion, who *was* he? But if there was one thing he'd learned to do in life it was to roll with whatever punches fate dealt him.

"I've adjusted," he said. "Besides, working as the assistant foreman on the Rocking C pays the bills."

"So you rode broncs when you were on the circuit?" Anna asked.

Nate had never been one to toot his own horn, so he didn't mention the buckles he'd won. Instead, he just nodded and said, "Yep."

"No wonder you seemed so competent working with that gelding."

Horses, broken or not, he could handle. It was only little babies that made him uneasy.

And pretty social workers.

He shot a glance her way. Damn, she was attractive. And in spite of his better judgment, he was drawn to her. Her floral scent—gardenia maybe?—snaked around him and seemed to hold him captive. Just walking next to her was a pleasure.

But Anna Reynolds wasn't like the buckle bunnies who'd once hovered around him, hoping for a date, a kiss or…a whole lot more. She wasn't here to flirt or…whatever. She had a job to do—and possibly an assessment to make.

"What is it that you wanted to talk to me about?" he asked, hoping she'd cut to the chase and he could get his mind back on his work. "Is there a problem?"

"No, not that I see so far."

"Then why are you here?"

"It's my job to check up on you and the baby. Would it be easier for you if I came back in the evening next time?"

"Actually, this isn't a bad time. I'm sorry if it sounded like I was…" He paused, choosing his words carefully. "I was just a little surprised to see you this afternoon. That's all."

She blessed him with a pretty smile, one that he'd be thrilled to see if they'd met in a bar or honky-tonk, like the Stagecoach Inn. But could he trust that she didn't have any ulterior motives, other than to answer his questions and help him adjust to fatherhood? He'd been in the foster care system. He knew better than to take kindness at face value. Maybe he ought to try a little charm on her, knock her a little off balance.

"It's nice of you to come all the way out here to

check on us," he said, adding a carefree smile that was more fake than real.

"I'm just doing my job. Do you have any questions for me? Not just about babies, but about the social services available to you?"

He had plenty of questions. And the longer he was around little Jessie, the more he seemed to have. Like how much formula should she be taking at one time? Or why did it take so long to get a burp out of her? And was she going through too many diapers?

Instead, he said, "There's a nurse on duty at the ranch at all times, as well as the housekeeper. So they've been very helpful." In fact, they were far more capable of caring for a baby than he was.

Not that he expected Joy, Shannon and the other women to do it all for him. He hadn't left Jessie completely in their care. Hell, he practically hovered over her whenever he was in the house.

When Anna didn't smile or appear to be the least bit relieved by his admission, he added, "You don't need to worry." Especially about *me*. "We're doing fine."

"I'm sorry, Mr. Gallagher. I'm a little confused. I realized you mentioned staying here for a while—before taking her home. But do you have a place of your own?"

Did it matter? What was she really asking? Did she want to know if he could financially support a baby? Or was she worried that he wasn't able to provide a home for her?

"I own a house in Brighton Valley, but I'm staying

here for now. Jessie has a cradle in the office, and I sleep on the sofa." He felt as though he'd been caught in a lie, but it was the truth.

"That's good. I was going to ask if you needed my help finding a place."

"No, I've got that covered." Did she get this involved with other people on her caseload?

"When do you plan to take her home?" Anna asked.

"Soon." Now that was a lie. Just the thought of being alone with her scared the hell out of him.

But since Anna would undoubtedly come back to visit and would still find him at the ranch, he'd better clarify things now. "Before I take her home, I'll have to hire a nanny to watch her during the day so I can work. And I'm not ready to let a stranger take care of her yet. Besides, over the past few months, I've gotten to know the people who work with me here. They're almost like family, especially Sam the foreman and Joy the cook. The nurses are not only loving and kind, but they know what to do with a baby."

She tilted her head and frowned—maybe from the sunlight in her eyes. Still, it prompted him to add, "I'm learning a lot from the nurses about the baby. So no worries."

"I'm glad to hear things are going well," Anna said, although she crossed her arms and scanned the length of him as if she wasn't quite convinced. "I'd better let you go back to work. I'll see you again in a couple of days."

"Why?"

"It's my job. Remember?"

If she were anyone else, if she had any other job, he'd be pleased as punch to have her stop by—with or without notice. It was only the fear factor that had him uneasy, the concern that she might find him lacking as a father. And after this exchange, he had a feeling she'd pegged him as the phony he truly was.

But maybe he'd been making a much bigger deal out of her visits than he should have been. Maybe she'd been telling him the truth when she'd said she only wanted to be helpful.

"You have my number," she said.

"You bet I do." He tapped the front pocket of his shirt. Ever since she'd given it to him at the hospital, he'd decided to carry it with him at all times.

He might not want to have a social worker checking up on him, but that didn't mean he was too stubborn to call for help if he really needed it.

On Monday afternoon, after a long morning spent in meetings, followed by several visits with different parents in the NICU, Anna climbed into her car and headed to the red brick building that housed several medical offices, including Brighton Valley Pediatrics. She wasn't sure if Nate would be happy to see her or not, but she wanted to attend Jessica's first appointment.

Preemies could present a few additional problems and worries, something Anna knew firsthand. Five years ago, while she was in her last year of grad school, her mother remarried and then, six months later, gave birth to a second daughter. Kylie, Anna's sister, had been born ten weeks early and had faced several health issues. Fortunately, she was doing well now, but those early months had been very stressful and worrisome for everyone involved.

However, the real reason Anna had taken a special interest in Nate's case was because she'd recently faced the biggest failure of her career. Last spring, little Danny Walker had been born full-term, but he'd had a serious heart defect that required surgery. Sadly, his mother never bonded with him, and as a result, Danny had failed to thrive.

The situation was complicated by the fact that there'd been both a surrogate and a sperm donor involved. So in Danny's case, no one had been fully committed to raising a fragile child.

Once Danny had gone into foster care, his health improved and he began gaining weight. His prognosis was good, and the last she'd heard, he'd been cleared for adoption. But she would always regret not picking up on the warning signs and facilitating his placement sooner. That's why Nate's case was so important to her and why she would do everything in her power to help him bond with his daughter. If he didn't…

Well, if he showed signs of not taking proper care of her or providing her the loving home she both needed and deserved, Anna would have the baby removed from his care.

As the elevator doors opened and let her out on the third floor, a little zing rushed through her bloodstream, kicking her pulse up a notch. Okay, so she had to admit that she was also drawn to the handsome daddy for another reason, one that had nothing to do with his parenting skills. But even so, that had nothing to do with her hope to see him become a great dad.

At least, she certainly hoped it didn't.

She glanced at her wristwatch. It was 4:06. She'd wanted to arrive at the pediatric office a little earlier than this. Would she find Nate still in the waiting room? Or had he already been called back for the weigh-in?

Her question was answered the moment she scanned the room and saw the new daddy sitting near an aquarium, the baby carrier on his lap, his black Stetson on the chair next to him. He glanced up about the same time she spotted him.

He tossed her a crooked grin that darn near turned her heart inside out and stirred up a swarm of butterflies in her stomach. Okay, so her gut wasn't the only thing sending feelings about Nate to her brain. But she'd have to tuck that emotional stuff away. She wasn't about to breach any ethical boundaries by letting the sight of Nate Gallagher in those jeans and boots get to her.

Maybe she should come up with an excuse to say hello, then leave and let him visit the doctor on his own.

Yet in spite of her second thoughts, her feet seemed to move toward him on their own. So she blew off her fluttery tummy and tamped down her thumping heart.

His lips tilted into the slightest of smiles. "I wasn't sure if you'd show up."

Had he hoped that she would? It certainly sounded that way.

"I'm glad you came," he added.

Seriously? For some reason, his admission stirred up that flock of butterflies that had begun to settle down during her walk across the room.

Oh, for Pete's sake, he hadn't meant anything by that. He was a new father, worried about his newborn and eager to learn whether she'd gained weight.

But even that realization didn't help. After all, Danny Walker's parents had charmed her into thinking they were glad that she'd come by to see their baby, yet their smiles and affirmations had just been a show. They'd rarely even held that little boy.

Deciding that she'd made an unfair comparison, Anna shook off the memory. "As it turned out, I was able to get off work on time." She glanced into the carrier at Jessica, who was as precious as could be in a pink sleeper that was way too large for her small size.

Her dark hair was adorned with a white bow attached to a headband, and while her eyes remained closed, her lips moved as though nursing on a bottle or pacifier.

"She's got to be the cutest baby ever," Anna said. "Did you dress her?"

"Nope." Nate, who'd been studying the newborn, looked up and added, "Even if I felt comfortable doing that sort of thing, I didn't stand a chance. Jessie's gotten pretty popular with the nursing staff."

"I can certainly see why. But you're not comfortable dressing her?" Another red flag flapped in her mind.

Before he could answer, the back door opened to reveal an older woman wearing a light blue smock with a zoo animal print. "Jessica Gallagher?" she called.

"That's us." Nate got to his feet and turned to Anna. "Did you want to wait here or come inside?"

Right this moment, there wasn't anything she wanted more than to join him in the exam room. And for that reason, as well as those pesky butterflies in her belly, she decided she'd better let Nate go in alone. "You go ahead. I'll be here when you get back."

"Okay." He nodded toward the Stetson on the chair. "Watch my hat?"

"You bet."

But it was the new daddy holding his newborn in the carrier she was more intent upon watching as he sauntered across the floor with a sexy cowboy swagger.

Still, there seemed to be something missing, something Nate was keeping from her. And she was determined to find out just what it was.

For everyone's sake.

Nate followed the nurse back to the exam room.

"How's it going?" she asked.

"Okay, I guess."

She pointed to the doorway of a room that had a medical smell, one that reminded him of those days he'd spent in the hospital. The familiar scent threw him even more off balance than when he'd first arrived.

"You want me to take her out of this contraption?" Nate asked, assuming he'd have to.

"Yes. Then get her undressed so I can weigh her."

Great. Nate had changed Jessica's diaper before—several times. And once, when she'd spit up all over them both, he'd had to put her in new jammies—or whatever it was called. But that didn't mean he felt comfortable moving her little arms and legs around. Still, he supposed the old adage was true. Practice made perfect.

"I just fed her," he told the nurse. "So her weight could be up because of that. But I also changed her in the waiting room."

"It all balances out," she said.

When Nate removed all but her diaper, Jessie let out a wail as though he'd hurt her.

"Goodness," the nurse said, as if screaming, red-faced newborns with flailing arms and legs were a common occurrence. "Would you listen to that? She's certainly got a temper and a strong pair of lungs."

As the woman started toward the door with Jessie in her arms, she turned to Nate. "Are you coming with me to the scale?"

"Absolutely." The whole point of today's doctor visit was to make sure her weight was on target.

He followed her to another room, this one smaller than the other. There she proceeded to weigh an unhappy Jessie.

He held his breath as he waited to hear the result. What in the world was he going to do if she hadn't gained any weight? Or worse, what if she'd lost a few ounces?

But then the nurse looked up and smiled. "Good job, Daddy! She's up nearly six ounces since she was discharged from the hospital."

Nate's heart soared as if he could take all the credit himself. And even though he'd only played a small role, he felt as if he'd just gone eight seconds on a bronc no one could ride.

He wished Anna could have been standing here, hearing the news herself, but he supposed that it was just as well that she'd remained in the waiting room. He was still a little uneasy around her and didn't want her to pick up on his insecurities or to know how far out of his element he really was.

Five minutes later, after the doctor had examined Jessie and declared her healthy and thriving, Nate redressed her with minimal issues and secured her into the carrier. Then he returned to the waiting room feeling far more competent than when he'd arrived.

Anna, who was still seated in the same chair, set the magazine she'd been reading aside, reached for her purse and got to her feet. "How'd it go?"

"Great. She's gained six ounces already, which is almost a half pound. So that's a relief."

"I'm sure it is. Now you can go home and celebrate."

As much as he missed his privacy, he wouldn't be going back to his house. He still wanted to stick close to the Rocking C, although he felt much better about things now.

"I guess there's a lot to be happy about, but I won't be celebrating the way I used to. Something tells me that having a couple of beers with my friends at the Stagecoach Inn won't be appropriate. But I'll probably stop by Caroline's Diner for dinner and splurge on dessert."

"That might be a lot more fun, especially with a baby."

As they started toward the door, he found himself asking, "Are you hungry?"

The question seemed to take her aback because her eyes widened and her lips parted. But before he could renege on the implied invitation, she said, "Actually, I had a light lunch, so yes, I *am* hungry."

He supposed it was too late to backpedal now. "Do you want to meet me at Caroline's?"

"Sounds like a plan."

Yep, he supposed it did. Hopefully, it didn't also sound like a date. He opened the door for the pretty social worker then followed her out.

Not that dating Anna Reynolds wouldn't be appealing. But Nate wasn't about to get romantically involved with someone who could stir up trouble.

Or worse, someone with the power to take Jessie away from him.

Chapter Three

By the time Nate arrived at Caroline's Diner and found a parking space in front, Jessie had fallen back asleep, thank goodness. It nearly killed him to hear her cry, which she'd started to do as soon as they'd exited the doctor's office.

After unhooking the car seat from the base, he carried her to the diner entrance then waited for Anna, who was locking up her car, to join them.

"I've never been here before," Anna said. "But I've heard a lot of good things about it."

"Every single one is true. Caroline makes the best food in town." Nate opened the glass door, setting off the jangle of a bell, and stood aside, waiting for Anna to enter.

He knew he had to be on guard when he was

around her, but the more time he spent with her, the more he began to think she'd been telling the truth when she'd said she only wanted to help.

Maybe having dinner together this evening would ease his nervousness around her and make him feel better about asking her questions and seeking advice.

Or would she pump him for information? Had she started listing things in her file until she had reason to take Jessica away?

Maybe he was just being paranoid. She didn't seem like the sort of person to do that.

He cut a glance at her profile, watched as she scanned the interior of the small-town eatery, with its pale yellow walls and white café-style curtains on the front windows, then focused on the refrigerator display case that sat next to the old-fashioned register. As usual, it was filled with a variety of homemade desserts.

Nate had always had a sweet tooth and was eager to sample one of the pies—looked like they had banana cream again today, which was his favorite. But then again, maybe he'd have a slice of that three-layer carrot cake.

"What's that mean?" Anna pointed out the blackboard that advertised the daily special.

As usual, *What the Sheriff Ate:* was written in yellow chalk. Today that was followed by *Tri Tip, Mashed Potatoes and Gravy, Green Beans, Butter Horn Rolls and Lemon Meringue Pie.*

"Caroline's husband is retired now," Nate explained, "but he was once the only law enforcement officer in

Brighton Valley. So she and almost everyone in town still refer to him as 'the sheriff.'"

Margie, who'd worked as a waitress at the diner for as long as Nate could remember, must have heard the bell at the door jangle. Her jovial voice called out from the back room, "Y'all don't need to wait to be seated. Take any table you like. I'll be with you in a minute."

Obviously, she hadn't seen Nate yet, which was just as well. Margie was a nice lady, but as curious as heck and a real talker. The minute she spotted the baby and Anna, she was going to give him the third degree.

Maybe he'd luck out and get one of the newer—and quieter—waitresses, although that wasn't likely. And even if it was, Margie always made the rounds, checking on all of the diners.

"Come on," Nate said. "Let's sit in that back corner booth."

They'd no more than taken a seat and placed the baby carrier between them when Margie stopped by the table with two menus. Her ruddy complexion gave way to a shock of graying dark hair, piled high on her head. The moment she recognized Nate, she offered him a bright-eyed grin. "Well, if it isn't our favorite bronc rider."

At one time, Nate might have beamed at the compliment, but he was no longer on the circuit, and his heart ached at the reminder. He'd learned to deal with it, or so he'd thought, but every once in a while the loss snuck up on him like a charging bull and gored him in the gut.

"Thanks," he said, "but I'm just a cowhand these days."

"Oh, pshaw. You'll always be a champ to me—and to the other folks in town." Margie winked, then glanced at Anna, taking time to size her up good.

Nate opened his menu and pretended to study his choices, even though he'd already decided what he wanted before he entered the diner. He hoped the sweet but curious waitress would go on about her business. But apparently, he wasn't going to be that lucky.

"You doin' okay now?" Margie asked him. "Sam was in here a couple of days ago, along with Joy, that pretty gal of his. He told me that you've been released from physical therapy."

Sam didn't have a big mouth and didn't spread rumors, but apparently, he opened up when pressed. Margie, bless her sweet, gossip-prone heart, had a way of mining information from everyone in town then connecting her own dots.

"Yep," Nate said. "They turned me loose. So no worries. I'm doing fine."

In a physical sense, that was true. He could still walk and even line dance if he got the whim, but his career options had been severely limited by the accident. He slid his hand over his right hip, the one the docs rewired and bolted back together.

Margie brightened then turned to Anna. "Well, hello there, hon. I didn't mean to ignore you. It's just that Nate here has been on everyone's prayer list ever since that bronc darn near stomped him to death."

Nate tensed. Dammit. Why'd she have to bring that up here—and now?

As if the news of the accident passed right by her, Anna introduced herself.

"It's nice to meet you," Margie said, glancing first at Nate, then at Anna and back to him again. The false assumption she'd made was obvious.

Before Nate could correct her, Jessie let out a cry, and Margie began to connect a whole lot of dots that didn't exist.

"Oh, my gosh," the waitress said. "Who is this sweet little thing?"

"This is Jessica," Anna said. "She's Nate's daughter."

Margie's eyes widened, and her jaw dropped. In fact, if someone had thrown a soaring plastic disc her way, she could have caught it in her mouth. "Well, now, isn't that nice."

Nate had half a notion to object, to clarify how this had all come to be, to offer up the truth of the matter. After all, his name might be on Jessie's birth certificate, but he wasn't so sure he was actually her father.

As a multitude of explanations rose up, he clamped his mouth shut. No one needed to know his thoughts and fears. Besides, other than him, who else did she have?

As far as anyone needed to know, he *was* Jessie's daddy.

Before he could ponder just how much he wanted

Margie—and therefore the entire town—to know, Margie clapped her pudgy hands together and broke out in a big old grin. "Well, I'll be darned. Nate Gallagher got married. That bit of news is going to break the hearts of all the single girls in town."

"I'm afraid you misunderstood," Anna said. "We're not married."

Margie's graying brows shot up, and she covered her mouth with the fingers of her right hand. "Oops. I just assumed…?" She glanced at Nate, clearly chumming for a better explanation.

He'd be damned if he wanted to give her one. This particular waitress was the last person in Brighton Valley he'd want to know his business, even if she was making false assumptions right and left.

When Margie realized Nate wasn't offering up the info she'd wanted, she said, "Either way, you two have a beautiful little baby. She's absolutely precious."

"She's not mine," Anna said.

Margie's forehead creased, and she took a closer peek at Jessie. "Are you sure about that? She looks a lot like you."

The hell she did. And what mother in the world wouldn't know whether a baby was hers or not?

Anna shot a glance at Nate. She didn't have to utter a single word. He could read her question in her eyes: *What are you going to do to set this woman straight?*

Damn, but he hated to go into detail. He was still pondering an explanation when Margie gasped, "Oh, my! Is that the little baby whose poor mama died a few weeks back?"

* * *

Anna waited for Nate to respond, although he seemed to have clammed up. She, as well as everyone at the hospital and at the sheriff's office, had been aware of the tragic details surrounding Elizabeth Huddleston's death. So it wasn't any surprise that people in the local diner knew about the woman who'd suffered a severe beating, had gone into premature labor and later died.

Did they also know that, after the assault, Elizabeth had somehow managed to drive to the Rocking C? Anna assumed the injured woman had gone in search of Nate, although that was just a guess on her part.

Shannon Cramer, the head nurse at the ranch, had called the paramedics, and Ms. Huddleston had been rushed to the hospital in time to give birth. Fortunately, the baby, who was born six weeks early, hadn't had any serious complications. That is, other than the loss of her mother.

Two different legal proceedings had followed, one of which led to the arrest of the woman's husband. The other gave Nate custody of the baby. But it wasn't Anna's place to respond to the questions of the inquisitive waitress, so she waited for Nate to answer.

He finally sighed and cleared his throat. "Yes, Margie. This is the baby. But under the circumstances, I'd like to keep that quiet. You know how people around town can talk, and I don't want this innocent little girl to carry a burden like that, especially while she's so young."

The defense of his daughter touched Anna in an unexpected, heart-stirring way. How could it not? She stole a glance at the chatty waitress, whose expression and misty eyes suggested she, too, sympathized with the baby's plight.

"Don't worry, Nate." Margie reached into the front pocket of her yellow apron, pulled out a wadded-up tissue and used it to blot her tears. "That poor, precious little girl."

Nate struck a casual pose, resting his forearms on the table. "I know it won't be easy for you to keep a secret like that, Margie. With so many people coming in and out of the diner, there's bound to be talk. But I'd really appreciate it if you didn't…you know, help things along."

"I won't say a word." Margie lifted her right hand as if she were in a courthouse, about to take the witness stand. "I'd never do anything to hurt a child, especially one who's been dealt such a cruel blow already. You can count on me to keep quiet about that."

"You're a good-hearted woman," Nate said. "I never doubted that."

Margie glanced at the baby then back at Nate. "I heard that it was the woman's husband who beat her up. How did you…? Well, since y'all said the baby is yours, I just wondered how…that happened."

Nate tensed, and Anna didn't blame him. She'd had the same question herself, but voicing it, even in a nearly empty diner, was in poor taste and completely out of line. Still, Anna couldn't help waiting for his response. Had he been having an affair with a married woman?

"Just for the record," Nate said, "Jessie's mother was single when she and I dated."

To Margie's credit, her cheeks flushed bright pink. "Oh, goodness, Nate. I never meant to imply that you'd… Well, it's just so sad, that's all."

When Nate didn't respond, Margie placed her hand on his shoulder. "I'm sorry for your loss, darlin'. It must have ripped your heart right out to lose your sweetheart and your baby's mama, especially with her dying the way she did."

Rather than address Margie's comment or her sympathy, Nate said, "I don't suppose we could bother you for two cups of coffee."

Margie straightened then seemed to pull it all together. "Yes. Of course. Coming right up."

When Nate and Anna were finally alone in the corner booth, he continued to lean forward, his forearms resting on the table, his clasped hands on top of the menu, and said, "You might not like coffee or feel up to having any right now, but I needed to change the subject and give her a reason to move on."

Anna placed her fingers over the top of his knuckles, an intimate reaction that took her by surprise. But she shared her remorse and an apology anyway. "I'm sorry, Nate. I have a feeling that's something you'd wanted to keep to yourself. So I'm sorry if I said or implied anything that might have stirred her curiosity."

"You didn't." He shrugged a single shoulder.

"Sooner or later that news was going to get out anyway. Everyone at the Rocking C already knows. Not that any of them are talkers, but...well, some secrets are hard to keep."

Anna understood why he'd want to keep the tragic news about Jessie's mother from a woman who was undoubtedly prone to passing along community news, even if it only amounted to gossip. But he was right. This was the kind of thing people naturally wanted to ponder, speculate and share.

"Just for the record," Nate added, his sky blue eyes locking on to Anna's and stirring up an emotion of some kind, one she couldn't quite put her finger on, "I'm really not grieving for Beth. Not the way you or Margie might think. I mean, I feel bad about what happened to her. She was a nice woman, but we weren't...very close. It's Jessie who's really going to miss her. A girl needs a mother."

That was true. At times, while Anna had been growing up, she'd wished she had a mother like some of her friends. But Sharon Reynolds had been too young and self-centered to step up and be a strong feminine role model. Not that the two of them had any lingering relationship problems. They were actually somewhat close now, even though Sharon had yet to fully grow up. In fact, to this day, she acted more like a big sister—one that could be a bit wild and reckless at times. Thank goodness her new husband could afford a nanny to take care of Kylie and to handle most of the day-to-day parenting issues.

A girl needs a mother.

Anna glanced across the table, where Nate stared down at the closed menu in front of him, a crease marring his handsome brow. A girl needed a father, too.

Was he worried that he might not measure up to what his daughter was going to require in the future? Was he afraid that she or others might find him lacking?

"Daddies are important to little girls, too," she said.

Nate lifted his head, his gaze seeking out hers. He didn't comment right away, but when he did, his voice was low and soft. "They're also important to little boys."

She tried to read the subtext behind his words and assumed he might have a few daddy issues, just like she did. She didn't talk about them anymore, hoping they'd just fade away. But thanks to a nearly nonexistent relationship with the man who'd abandoned her as a child, they always seemed to be hiding under the surface, ready to pop up like an annoying jack-in-the-box when she least expected them to.

Sure, as a licensed social worker, she was trained to spot those things in others. But it wasn't always easy to recognize them in herself.

She studied the man across from her, and while she'd meant to observe him as a daddy, her thoughts drifted from those meant to be professional to others more personal. In spite of her best efforts, she found herself observing him as a man—and a very attractive one at that.

His brown hair, which had a slight indention from where his hat once rested, nearly shouted cowboy, even without his Stetson. His eyes were a pretty shade of blue, the color of bluebonnets growing in a meadow. Yet that was the only thing "pretty" about him. He was both rugged and handsome, something she found far more appealing than she'd expected to—and way more than she should.

Jessica squirmed again, scrunched her little face and began to fuss, this time sounding irritable—and hungry. Anna had never been one to let a baby cry, but this time, tending to the little girl's needs quickly would allow her to change her focus, to get her thoughts back on an appropriate track.

"It sounds like she's hungry," Anna said. "Would you like me to feed her?"

"Sure." Nate's response came out quickly, nearly sparking with enthusiasm. Then, as if catching himself, he added, "That is, if you want to."

Actually, she should let him do it so she could observe his interaction with the baby, but it was too late to backpedal now. "Of course."

Nate reached into the black canvas tote he used as a diaper bag and whipped out a small plastic bottle with premeasured dry formula. Next he withdrew a container of water.

While he unscrewed the lids and mixed the two together, Anna removed Jessie from the carrier and cuddled her in her arms. She felt warm and soft—so sweet and vulnerable. Her baby powder scent triggered a protective streak, something Anna hadn't felt with the other infants on her caseload. Sympathy, she supposed, for a child who didn't have a mother.

She cooed to the little one, shushing her and swaying as though seated in a rocking chair and not a booth in a small-town diner.

"Here you go," Nate said, handing over the bottle.

Within seconds, as Jessie suckled the nipple as if there were no tomorrow, an unexpected warmth filled Anna's chest and brought a smile to her face.

How odd, she thought. She'd fed babies before, but this tiny little girl who'd lost her mommy was stirring something deep within, something soft and tender. She wasn't sure what to call it. A maternal longing?

No, it couldn't be that. Not when Anna's biological clock hadn't even started ticking.

When Margie returned for their orders—a hearty bacon cheeseburger and fries for Nate and a grilled chicken salad for Anna—the friendly waitress took a moment to marvel at the baby before disappearing into the kitchen.

By the time their meals were served, Jessica had downed nearly the entire bottle, as small as it was, burped and dozed off again.

After securing the sleeping infant back in her carrier, Anna picked up a fork and speared a piece of grilled chicken out of her salad while Nate took a bite of his juicy burger. They ate in silence for a while, although she stole a glance across the table every now and again. A couple of times she caught Nate looking at her.

Finally, when she'd eaten her fill, she blotted her

lips with the napkin. "That was amazingly good. I'd heard a lot of good things about this diner, so it's been on my list of local restaurants to try."

"I told you Caroline's is the best." Nate tossed her a charming but playful smile. "That is, if you're into down-home cooking. Some people claim it's 'better than mama can make.'"

"It was certainly better than anything my mom has ever cooked or baked." Anna's mother had always relied on canned soup and boxed macaroni and cheese—and probably still did. But at least it was filling.

"I don't remember my mom," Nate said. "She died of breast cancer before I entered kindergarten."

"I'm so sorry to hear that." Anna might not have had the best mother in the world, but at least she'd had one. "It must have been tough on you and your father."

Nate shrugged. "My dad had a drinking problem to begin with. And rather than working through his grief, he tried to drown it."

A second round of "I'm sorry" wasn't going to fly, so Anna just listened, waiting for him to go on. When it seemed as if he might not go into any more detail, she asked, "Does he still drink?"

"I don't know. He took off when I was thirteen, and I haven't seen him since."

Anna's compassion for the small boy who'd lost his mother and had been left in the care of an alcoholic dad stirred up a slew of emotions, including her worry for little Jessie. Nate clearly hadn't had a paternal role model. Would he be able to provide Jessie with what she needed?

Sure, Anna hadn't gotten the best role models herself. Her parents had been young and had fought more than they got along. Actually, when they finally split up, creating peace in the home, Anna had been relieved. But at least she'd had a mother, albeit one that had been far from perfect. She'd also taken a lot of psychology courses in college, which helped her to understand people and various family dynamics.

Now, here she was in Brighton Valley, creating a life for herself. She had a job she loved, although she'd always dreamed of creating the perfect family. She was just waiting for the right man to come along.

She stole a glance at the cowboy seated across from her. In spite of her attraction, he wasn't her Mr. Right, so she wouldn't entertain that thought for a moment.

There was also plenty for her to be concerned about in this case, and she planned to give it her top priority, even if that meant checking on the cowboy daddy when she wasn't on the clock.

"Are you ready to go?" Nate asked.

She nodded and reached for her purse. He grabbed the handle of the baby carrier, then they slid out of the booth and walked to the front of the diner. They stopped by the register to pay the bill.

Margie, who met them there, rang up the charge. "That'll be twenty-three dollars and sixteen cents."

Anna reached into her purse, pulled out a twenty and handed it to Nate.

He put up his hand and refused it. "Put your money away. I've got this."

"Oh, no, you don't." There was no way she'd let him pay for her dinner. "I expected this to be Dutch treat."

"Actually, the payment logistics were never decided." Nate handed Margie two twenties. "I asked you to join me, remember? Besides, it's the cowboy way."

Anna wasn't sure what he meant by that. But rather than ask him to explain, she said, "Okay, but I'll get it…next time." Darn it. She hadn't meant to imply that they'd have dinner together again.

As if her comment hadn't struck him the least bit presumptive, he said, "It's a deal."

"And, Nate, don't worry." Margie lowered her voice as she counted out the change. "I won't say a word about *you-know-who*. Or about *you-know-what*."

"I'd appreciate that." Nate offered the waitress a ten-dollar tip. "That's for you."

Margie brightened. "Why, thank you, hon."

It seemed more like a bribe to Anna than a tip, but maybe Nate was just a generous man.

With the strap of the diaper bag over his shoulder and the baby carrier in one hand, he opened the front door for Anna with the other.

On the way out, Anna again pondered what he'd meant when he'd said paying for her dinner tonight was "the cowboy way." Common courtesy, she supposed. Good manners and generosity.

Rather than split up and each go their own way, Nate walked her to her car.

"Thanks for dinner," she said.

"My pleasure." A glimmer lit his blue eyes, one that almost seemed flirtatious, and she nearly forgot who he was—and why it wasn't a good idea to let silly, girlish attraction get the better of her.

She continued to stand there, under the streetlight with the handsome bronc rider, caught up in what appeared to be a romantic moment with a man who lived by some kind of cowboy creed.

His ideals intrigued her.

He intrigued her.

In fact, she'd gotten a new perspective about rodeos and ranchers this evening, which was weird. She'd never been attracted to that kind of man before, although she really couldn't say why. Maybe because she'd grown up in the city. But right this minute, she felt inclined to reconsider her stand on dating cowboys.

And why was that? She didn't get involved with country boys—or with people she needed to help and support through her job.

"G' night," he said, revealing a soft Southern twang she hadn't noticed before. "Drive carefully."

She nodded and climbed into her car before she said or did anything to give in to her inappropriate thoughts.

But as she backed out of the parking space, she couldn't help looking in the rearview mirror and stealing one last peek at Cowboy Daddy—and saw him watching her go.

* * *

Nate stood outside Caroline's Diner until Anna had backed out of her parking space and was driving down Brighton Valley's main drag. It had been an interesting night, and for a while he'd nearly forgotten who Anna was and why she'd met him at the pediatrician's office.

He hadn't planned to ask her to join him for dinner, but the idea had rolled off his tongue as if it was the most natural thing in the world for them to do. Once the words were out, he'd expected her to gracefully decline, but she hadn't, which surprised him.

Several times, when they'd been seated in that corner booth, he'd had to remind himself of the trouble she could cause him, especially if she knew that a DNA test might prove he wasn't Jessie's father. And what would happen when she realized he didn't know squat about small children, especially baby girls?

Still, even though he'd been on high alert, she'd managed to draw something out of him, a memory he'd hinted at and nearly revealed. One he kept under wraps because it would be too painful to let it out into the light of day.

Over the years, life had thrown a lot of curves his way, beginning with the death of his mother when he'd barely been five. As if that hadn't been bad enough, he'd had to deal with an alcoholic father who'd taken to drinking himself to sleep each night. And when a case of beer no longer did the trick, he'd switched to straight Scotch.

When his old man lost his job, he couldn't pay

the rent or the power bill, which had led them to a church-run homeless shelter, where they'd stayed several nights—after a sermon and some prayers. Then one day, his dad set off to buy a pack of cigarettes and never returned.

When someone from the church realized Nate was alone, they called social services, and he ended up in foster care.

So that's why he was hell-bent on keeping Jessie from suffering the same type of fate. And that was also why he couldn't let Kenny's family take her. So he'd decided to do whatever he could to keep her safe and to provide some kind of home for her, just like his maternal grandpa had eventually done for him.

When his mom's father, retired rodeo champ Clinton McClain, first learned of Nate's plight, he'd gone to court and asked for custody. Then he'd brought Nate to live on the Double M Ranch. There, on the outskirts of Brighton Valley, Nate grew to manhood—and that was where he'd learned the cowboy way.

Be a man of integrity, Grandpa Clint had said. *Be honest, especially with yourself, and be true to your friends.*

Damn. He missed that ranch, too. But Grandpa Clint had sold it while Nate had been on the rodeo circuit without asking Nate if he'd be interested in buying it himself. He would have, but he'd never... well, he'd never thought he needed to. He'd just assumed that his grandfather knew how he felt about the Double M. Or how Nate felt about a lot of things, like the man he'd come to love and respect.

After Grandpa Clint died, Nate inherited the house in town, though. And last year, when the doctors told Nate he'd have to give up riding rodeo ever again, he'd moved in during his recovery period.

It had hurt giving up his rodeo dreams, but he was also grateful to be alive, so he sucked up his disappointment, just as he had his memories of a lousy childhood. Before long he began to put his own mark on the place on Peachtree Lane—like buying a new bedroom set and bedding, as well as new living room furniture.

Nate rubbed his hip, which ached from sitting, then glanced at the sweet baby dozing in the carrier. Before he knew it Jessie would be hungry again, so he'd better get her back to the ranch.

After securing her in the backseat of his pickup, he climbed behind the wheel and started the engine. But instead of heading for the county road that would take him to the Rocking C, he drove through town and turned onto Peachtree Lane.

He hadn't been home since Jessie was discharged from the hospital, and he missed his house, as well as his privacy.

As he pulled along the curb and parked under the streetlight, he took a good hard look at the white house, its green trim and black front door. Other than the grass, which needed to be mowed, it looked the same as when he'd left it. At least, it did on the outside.

If he didn't need to get Jessie home, he'd go inside for a while. He'd just begun to put his own mark on the place and was eager to finish what he'd started. But he wasn't about to move back home before Jessie got a little older and he found a competent, live-in nanny. So until then he was stuck on the Rocking C.

Maybe *stuck* wasn't exactly the right word to use. He enjoyed living on a ranch, but it wasn't the same as being on the Double M. Besides, with all the rodeo talk, it only served to remind him of all he'd lost.

He glanced at the clock on the dash—7:11 p.m. A lot of guys, especially those who frequented Las Vegas, would consider them lucky numbers. At one time Nate might have taken that as a sign that his once charmed life was back on track. Only trouble was, his old life was gone for good.

The accident had shattered his future, but with time and physical therapy, he'd recovered and was making the best of his lot in life. Then Beth had shown up on the Rocking C, claiming her baby was his. That unsettling news, along with his acceptance of it and his commitment to Jessie, had turned his world upside down again.

He just hoped Anna's offer to help him was sincere. Because if it wasn't, the complications would sweep over him and all he had left like a Texas twister, destroying everything in its path.

Chapter Four

It had been an exceptionally grueling day at work, and Anna was eager to go home. Soon after she'd started her shift this morning, a three-pound preemie had undergone emergency heart surgery. To make matters worse, the baby's parents had suffered several miscarriages before finally carrying a little girl for seven months. Needless to say, they were worried sick.

Anna had done her best to reassure the couple that the doctors were competent and that their daughter was in good hands, which was true. But complications could always arise.

Thankfully, all had gone well. The baby was back in the NICU now with her parents at her side.

Since Anna hadn't been able to take a lunch break,

she'd grabbed a protein bar from the break room on her way to an afternoon meeting with the nursing staff and Mary Grangetto, the new hospital administrator. Mary had a world of experience and would probably do a fine job overseeing the hospital, but she wasn't nearly as warm and understanding as the man she'd replaced.

By four o'clock that afternoon, Anna was ready to call it a day. The minute she arrived home, she planned to kick off her shoes and relax. She didn't feel up to cooking anything, but that wasn't a problem. She had fresh bread, deli meat and veggies. So she would make a sandwich for dinner, then she'd pour a glass of wine and escape by watching television.

Unfortunately, those plans were immediately dashed the minute she unlocked her front door and found the living room flooded, the carpet not just soaked, but also several inches under water.

Seriously? After the day I've already had, I had to come home to this?

She removed her shoes and left them on the porch. Then she went inside the house to determine the cause of the damage. Had she left a faucet running?

Surely she hadn't. She placed her purse and briefcase on the small table near the door then sloshed through an inch or two of cold water in her bare feet to check the kitchen and the bathroom.

She didn't find any of the faucets on, which meant she hadn't caused the problem, so she should feel relieved. But what was she supposed to do now?

First of all, she'd better alert her landlord, so she

returned to the living room, reached into her purse, pulled out her cell and dialed Carla Howard's number.

As soon as Carla answered, Anna said, "I'm afraid I have some bad news. I think we have a broken pipe. The entire house is flooded."

"Oh, no. I'll call a plumber, although..." Carla paused, as if concerned about something. "It's already after hours."

Anna glanced at her wristwatch. It was dinnertime on a Friday night. Then she looked down at her wet feet and gauged the water level. "Hopefully you can find someone with emergency hours. There's no way you can wait until Monday. The walls will be ruined."

"Don't worry. I'll figure out something. I also have a key, so if you have weekend plans, feel free to leave. I can meet the plumber."

"Actually, I don't have any plans. But..." Anna let out a little sigh. Turning in early was no longer going to be a possibility. "I'd better pack a bag and go somewhere. I can't stay here."

Carla clucked her tongue. "I'm sorry for this inconvenience, Anna. I'd offer to let you stay with me, but my sister and her family just arrived for a week-long visit."

That was just as well. Carla lived nearly an hour away, and Anna had to work a half day tomorrow.

"Would you mind staying at the Night Owl Motel for a day or two?" Carla asked. "My neighbor's son owns the place, so I can give him a call. I'll pay for your room, of course. And I'll have things all lined up before you arrive."

Anna thanked her, although she wasn't especially happy about staying at that particular place. Not that she didn't appreciate Carla's offer—or that she was picky and expected deluxe accommodations. It's just that the Night Owl was actually what she'd call a motor lodge located on a busy highway, right next to a truck stop and across the street from a cowboy bar called the Stagecoach Inn.

Since this was a Friday night, there was no telling how loud and rowdy things would get, and she'd had her heart set on having a quiet, restful evening. Of course, her options were now limited, so after the call ended, she packed her bag with two days' worth of clothing. Surely she wouldn't need more than a couple of outfits, a nightgown and undies. Then she gathered her toiletries together, snatched her purse from the living room table, locked up the house and returned to her car.

Ten minutes later she arrived at the Night Owl, tired and hungry. True to her word, Carla had called ahead of time and prepaid for a two-night stay.

"Here you go." The motel desk clerk handed her an old-fashioned key with a black plastic fob that had a faded gold ten stamped on it.

Anna thanked the balding, sixtysomething man then walked along the front of the white stucco building, searching each blue door for a number ten.

She'd no more than found the right room when her stomach growled, reminding her she'd missed the lunch meal and that it was well past the dinner hour. When she stuck the key into the lock, it opened right up.

The small room had a musty smell, and the furniture was dated. But it appeared to be clean. After unpacking, hanging her clothes in the dinky closet and putting away her toiletries in the bathroom, she went in search of a place to eat before the growls in her stomach became all-out roars.

Night was falling. The cars and big rigs whizzed by on the highway, most of their headlights turned on. So much for the quiet, cozy evening she'd planned.

Unless she wanted to get back in the car and drive across town, her dining choices were either the Stagecoach Inn or Joe's Café, which had a dangling orange neon sign announcing Good Eats.

She opted to cross the street and eat at the honky-tonk so she could order a glass of wine. Then she would order something to go and take it back to her room. Maybe she could still get that good night's sleep she'd hoped for—if that could be had in this part of town.

Once she opened the door of the local watering hole, she was met with hoots of laughter and the sounds of a country-western song playing on a red-and-chrome jukebox in the back. She almost turned around and headed back across the street to the café, but she'd come this far already. So she clutched the shoulder strap of her purse a little tighter and made her way across the scuffed, scarred hardwood floor to an Old West–style bar that stretched the length of the far wall.

She took a seat next to a couple of brunettes in their early twenties. Both women wore boots, jeans and snug T-shirts. One whispered something to the other, then they both burst into laughter.

About that time, the bartender, a blonde in her midforties, approached her with a smile. "Can I get you a drink?"

"I'd like a glass of Chardonnay. Do you have a wine list?"

"I'm afraid we're not that fancy. It's still happy hour, so the house white is half price. If you want the premium, it's..." She paused a moment and creased her brow. "You know, I'll have to check. It's something from California, I think. The new owner decided to offer a winery of the month special."

"Whatever it is, I'll have that." Anna wasn't what you'd call a wine connoisseur by any stretch of the word, but if she was going to take the time to unwind with a glass, she wanted it to be something good. "I'd also like to order a sandwich or something to go."

"You sure you don't want to stay and eat here? We're having a battle of the bands later this evening, and it's always fun when the dance crowd arrives."

"Thanks for the tip, but I...can't stay." Anna hoped things didn't get so loud and crazy that she'd hear it all the way across the street.

"Too bad. I'll be right back with a menu."

The bartender had no more than turned around when Anna thought she heard her ringtone. She pulled her cell phone from her purse and hurried to answer before the caller hung up.

"Hello?"

There was a mumble on the other end, so she pressed her cell phone against her ear, trying to block out the sounds of a Texas two-step as it blasted out of the jukebox.

The person—a male?—spoke again, calling her by name, but she didn't recognize the voice. Too bad she'd forgotten to look at the lighted display first.

"I'm sorry," she said. "I didn't catch that. Who is this?"

"Nate Gallagher. You said to call you anytime, but it sounds like you're too busy to talk."

"No, I'm not. It's just..." Darn it. With all the background noise—the laughter and music—he probably thought she was a party girl. But that couldn't be further from the truth.

"Why don't I call you tomorrow morning," he said.

"Oh, no." What if there was an emergency? What if he needed her—or rather, her advice or counsel. "This isn't a bad time for me. Just hold on a minute. Let me step outside where it's quiet."

She pushed her chair back and stood, but not before one of the brunettes called out, "I'll have another Jack Daniel's—straight up."

The bartender placed a glass of wine in front of Anna, a drink Anna no longer wanted, then told the brunette, "Coming right up."

Anna reached into her purse, pulled out a twenty and placed it on the bar so the bartender wouldn't think she'd abandoned her seat without planning to pay for her order.

"Put your money away." The bartender nodded toward the end of the bar, where a lanky cowboy sat, nursing a bottle of Budweiser and wearing a cocky smile. "That guy over there said to tell you that your drinks are on him tonight."

Oh, God. Did Nate hear that? If so, what must he think?

The cowboy lifted his bottle and winked at Anna.

"Thank him," Anna said, pressing the money into the waitress's hand, "but I won't be staying." At least, not any longer than it took to order a hamburger to go. She almost added that she bought her own drinks, but that was way more than she wanted Nate to hear. "I'll be back."

Then, without waiting for her change, she headed outside, hoping it would be quieter in the parking lot. And that in the cool of the evening, she could reestablish a more professional persona.

Nate pressed the phone to his ear, his fingers locked in a death grip. Anna had answered, but there was so much noise in the background—loud music, hoots and laughter—that he wasn't sure where she was. But she definitely wasn't at work.

He suspected it was a country-western bar because when she said she was going outside, where it was quiet, he could hear a familiar Toby Keith tune playing in the background.

Well, what do you know? There was a lot more to Anna Reynolds than met the eye. She hadn't come across as a woman who even knew how to kick up her heels before, but he now had reason to believe that he'd misjudged her.

The sound of a door creaked open then closed. When the background noise settled to a dull hum, Anna said, "Excuse me, Nate. I'm so sorry. I… Well, it's not…" She paused a moment, as if regrouping. Or was she trying to come up with a better explanation than the one she'd started to give him?

He didn't blame her for struggling with what to tell him. It really wasn't any of his business what she did with her spare time. Still, he found himself curious about the life Anna led when she wasn't working.

"Where are you?" he asked.

"I… Well, I could tell you that I'm attending an ice-cream social at the community church, but something tells me you wouldn't believe me."

He bit back a laugh, but couldn't stop a grin from spreading across his face. "No, that would be a real stretch—unless the church serves whiskey straight up while Toby Keith sings 'I Love This Bar.'"

"Okay, then. I'll answer honestly. I'm at the Stagecoach Inn. And for the record, I don't *love* this bar."

At that, he did laugh. When he managed to rein it in, he couldn't help asking, "Did you stop by after work? It sounds like you might have gone home first to change into boots, jeans and a hat."

"Would you believe I'm still in my business attire?"

"At a honky-tonk? No way. That sounds almost as far-fetched as the idea of you sitting on a bar stool while wearing a choir robe and eating a chocolate fudge sundae."

Her laugh, a soft lilt that struck an odd chord inside him, was drowned out by a big rig's air horn.

"It's a very long story," she said. "But it's the truth. My apartment flooded, and I have to spend the night at the Night Owl Motel. I was hungry and thought I'd order something to go. And the rest… Well, I suspect you heard plenty of it."

"If I were there, I'd offer to pay for your drinks all night, even if I had to fight the guy seated at the end of the bar."

"So you heard that, too?"

"Can't say as I'd blame him, whoever he is. In fact, if I didn't have a baby to worry about, I'd join you. Friday nights are a lot of fun at the Stagecoach Inn."

"Speaking of the baby," she said, "what's going on? Is everything okay? I assume you called me for a reason."

"It wasn't that important. I had a question to ask you and didn't stop to consider the time. I'll call you tomorrow, when you're on the clock…" He couldn't help adding, "And when you're not kicking up your heels at one of the favorite local bars."

"That's not why I'm here. And your call didn't bother me a bit. What was your question? And how can I help?"

The weird thing was, the question had been niggling at him ever since he first laid eyes on little Jessie, but it wasn't that critical to have an answer right now. It's not like he had any plans to leave the ranch for a while, but that didn't mean the question wasn't important.

"Actually," he said, "I'm wondering how to go about finding a qualified nanny or babysitter. I don't want to leave Jessie with just anyone. Besides, I want to do more than interview them or look over their list of references. I'm going to want someone to run a background check on them."

"It sounds like you're taking fatherhood seriously."

She had no idea how serious he was taking that role; how worried he was that he'd fumble the ball that had been tossed his way. But he didn't want her to think that he'd be a complete failure, especially when it came to finding the right sitter. "She's so small—and she can't talk. So she can't tell me if she's being mistreated or neglected."

"I can understand your concern," Anna said. "I have resource material back at the office. I'll bring it with me the next time I visit the ranch."

"Thanks. I'd appreciate that." It still didn't make him feel good about leaving a baby with a stranger. But he didn't want Anna to know how tightly his gut knotted at the thought of failing his…daughter. "I'd better let you go. I didn't mean to interrupt your Friday night."

"You're not bothering me," she said. "I told you before, I only stopped here to get something to eat."

Again, he couldn't help but tease her, to throw her off center for a change. "It's your story, Anna. Tell it any way you want."

"Believe it or not, I've never been one to frequent cowboy bars."

"Because you're not into cowboys?"

She paused a beat before answering. "You're never going to let me forget this, are you?"

Actually, he wasn't lying when he'd mentioned being at the Stagecoach Inn right now, seated with her. Listening to that old jukebox, throwing back a couple of ice-cold beers. Laughing, joking, dancing later on this evening. Maybe even taking her home with him…

But Anna wasn't the kind of woman he dated.

Although right now he wished she was.

By Monday afternoon Anna learned that her "two nights" at the Night Owl Motel had been extended to an indefinite stay. The plumber had found the problem easily enough, but correcting it was going to be a complicated process. There'd been a slow leak over a long period of time until the pipe had burst completely. As a result, they'd found mold in several walls.

The landlord had assured Anna that the insurance was handling everything and that the studio apartment would be back to normal soon. "In fact," Carla had added, "once the drywall guys get finished, the painters will come in. I've already picked out the carpet, although it's on backorder and won't be in for a week or two. But when we're done, it's going to seem like a brand-new house."

That was all well and good, but as a result, Anna wouldn't be returning home "soon."

After her workweek ended, she drove out to the Rocking C so she could check on Nate and Jessica. She also wanted to share the information she'd found for him. There was an agency in Wexler that vetted and supplied competent day-care workers. The only problem she could see would be the expense, which was probably pretty steep for a ranch hand's pay.

Now, as she waited at a stoplight, her blinker indicating her intention to turn right out of the medical center parking lot and onto the highway, she stretched her neck to one side and then the other, hoping to work out the pain and stiffness she'd woken up with this morning. In spite of the clean sheets, the bed at the Night Owl wasn't very comfortable.

Having to relocate, even for a few days, had been more than an unexpected inconvenience. She really liked her apartment, which was located near the hospital where she worked. It wasn't very big, and the furnishings weren't her own, but it was cute and cozy.

Of course, it wasn't very cute or cozy now. She'd stopped by earlier this morning to check on the workmen's progress, only to see it practically gutted, with an industrial-sized fan blowing against one wall.

What was she going to do if the removal of that mold took longer than originally expected? She'd have to find someplace else to rent—and that was going to take time.

So now here she was, waiting to pull into the intersection, one hand stifling a yawn and the other on the steering wheel. When the light turned green, she continued down the highway, turned on the radio and settled in for the drive to the Rocking Chair Ranch.

She told herself that she was making the evening visit to accommodate Nate's work schedule, which was true. But like it or not, there were a couple of other mitigating factors. One was to escape the sights and highway sounds near the motel. But the biggest reason, which she hated to admit, was a growing interest in Nate Gallagher. After their banter the other night, when he'd teased her about kicking up her heels at the Stagecoach Inn, she'd begun to…

No, she wasn't even going to consider having an attraction to the handsome cowboy. There was no way she'd act on any inappropriate feelings she might have for him. Not while he was a part of her caseload.

By the time Anna arrived at the ranch, it was nearly six o'clock and the sun had set. She parked her car then made her way to the front porch and knocked on the door.

The elderly ranch foreman answered, a grin stretching across his face. "What a surprise. You must be working the night shift."

Not really, but if Anna hadn't come this evening, she'd be watching TV in her motel room, the volume turned up to block out the sounds of traffic.

"Is Nate here?" she asked.

"Yep. Come on in." Sam stepped aside so she could enter. "He's got kitchen duty tonight."

Anna couldn't mask her surprise. "He made dinner?"

Sam laughed. "Are you kidding? We'd have a rebellion on our hands if Joy didn't cook for us. I just meant that Nate's stuck with the cleaning detail."

Anna scanned the large living room, where a group of oldsters were seated near the window. One of them was holding the baby, while the others oohed and aahed over her.

"I'll let Nate know you're here," Sam said.

Anna nodded then crossed the room to look in on little Jessie. The retired cowboy who was holding her glanced up and smiled. "She was fussing a few minutes ago, but once Joy changed her britches and wrapped her up like a little burrito, she settled right down."

"It's called swaddling," Anna said. "It keeps babies calm and content—and they like it."

"Until they get hungry or poop," one of the elderly men added. "Then all hell breaks loose."

Anna couldn't help but smile at the explanation—as well as the men's interest in the little girl.

"All right," a white-haired man said. "Don't be a baby hog, Raul. It's my turn to hold her."

"Like hell, Gilbert. You couldn't wait to pass her off to Joy the minute she started crying. You lost your turn."

"Yeah, but only long enough for Joy to change her diaper."

Anna hoped she'd get to see Nate argue for a chance to hold his daughter, to cuddle her. It was important for them to bond.

"Hey," a familiar deep voice said.

Speak of the handsome cowboy. Anna glanced over her shoulder to see Nate heading her way, his jeans worn but clean, his shirt neatly pressed, his hair damp as though he'd recently showered. For some reason, the sight of him and his sexy swagger chased away her professional reasons for a visit, replacing them with one that was far more personal.

Still, she offered a "Hey" right back at him.

He continued across the room, closing the distance between them until she picked up a whiff of masculine soap and the musky scent of his cologne. "I guess you weren't kidding when you mentioned coming to check on me in the evening."

Was that what he thought she was doing? Checking up on him, evaluating him?

That wasn't what she meant to do—or rather, it wasn't what she wanted him to think.

"I came by to follow up with you and make sure I'm doing everything I can to help. And I didn't want to bother you during your workday. I thought an evening visit would give us more time to talk." She hoped he was buying her explanation.

Nate glanced at the man holding the baby, his hands trembling slightly. Then he said, "Be careful there, Gilbert."

Gilbert frowned and drew the child closer to his chest. "I got her, Nate. It's not like I don't have any experience. Heck, I've had five of my own."

"Yes, but you said your kids were all born full-term and were twice her size." Something about the way Nate studied the tiny girl, the way he stood nearby as the shaky old man cuddled the flannel-wrapped bundle made Anna think he was coming around.

But she hadn't seen him hold his daughter yet, let alone give her a bottle. Surely he'd done so already—and often.

She knew that he was relying on the women at the ranch to help him for the time being. And, by the looks of it, the retired men were helping out, too. He'd also asked for Anna's advice on finding a qualified nanny, which meant he was concerned about Jessie's safety and care.

But a nanny was also just one more person for him to pass off the baby to.

"Do you want to talk in here?" Nate asked, drawing Anna from her speculation. "Or do you want to go out to the porch?"

The thought of speaking with him in private both pleased and unnerved her at the same time. Would she feel the same way if he were a homely cowboy who chewed tobacco and didn't feel the need for daily showers?

Now, there was a question that didn't need an answer.

"Sure," she said. "Let's go outside."

Nate nodded then headed out the door and onto the porch, with Anna tagging along behind him.

Going outdoors to talk with Nate was becoming a habit, it seemed. It was also an unfortunate one to foster. For a woman with a strong sense of ethics, she'd found herself looking forward to being alone with him entirely too much.

Chapter Five

Ever since Nate had placed that call to Anna and found her at the Stagecoach Inn, he'd begun to see her in a different light. Instead of a straitlaced professional in business attire, he envisioned her in a pair of fancy boots, tight jeans and a sexy T-shirt.

He'd once felt edgy and on guard around her, but that was no longer the case. Now he could easily imagine the two of them seated in a cozy, darkened booth at the local honky-tonk, toasting the evening by clinking one longneck bottle of beer against the other.

Or maybe she'd prefer a glass of wine.

He supposed her choice of drinks really didn't matter. Just the thought of them listening to country music and sharing a few laughs was enough to lighten his mood after he'd put in a hard day at work.

His tired, aching muscles no longer bothered him as they walked outside together, their way lit by the amber glow of the porch light. As they neared the barn they triggered the motion detectors, which instantly bathed the entire yard in light.

Unable to resist teasing her about her whereabouts on Friday night, Nate bumped his elbow against her arm. “I was a little surprised when you showed up after dinner this evening. I figured you'd prefer a more exciting place to wind down after work, maybe somewhere offering drinks, music and dancing.”

Anna froze midstep, slapped her hands on her hips and turned to face him, a crease in her brow. “I told you before. I wasn't hanging out at that bar. I just stopped in to order a hamburger to go.”

His smile deepened. “The Stagecoach Inn makes a mean burger. How'd you like it?”

“It was okay, I guess. But after all the ribbing you've been giving me, I wished I'd gone to Joe's Café and ordered a salad or sandwich instead.”

If she had, some of those lonely truckers who frequented Joe's would've been happy.

Anna started to walk again, and Nate fell in step beside her.

“Besides,” she said, “after the day I'd had at work, I wanted to unwind with a glass of wine. And I figured Joe only served coffee, tea and sodas.”

So that answered his question about her preferred drink.

“And for the record, I only had *one* glass,” she

added. "You may not believe this, but I've never been in a place like that before."

"No kidding?" Nate never had a problem getting information from a pretty lady he was attracted to. Not that he'd let his interest in this particular woman go any further than some flirtatious bantering. "That's a little surprising—for a Texas girl."

"I'm not from around here. I was born and raised in Oregon."

"Then why do I detect a soft Southern twang in your voice?"

She shot a glance his way, her brow scrunched again. "I don't have an accent."

"Actually, you do. But just a little one."

She seemed to think on that for a moment. "Maybe I picked it up from my mom. She was originally from Oklahoma."

Nate never let conversations drift toward family talk, which could open a can of memories he'd like to remain shut, so he steered the subject toward one that was a lot safer—and more lighthearted.

"So what'd you think of our local honky-tonk?" he asked.

"The Stagecoach Inn? I was only there for about fifteen minutes, but I guess it could make for an entertaining evening—if I hadn't been there alone."

He'd begun to think that Anna wasn't the kind of woman who should ever spend nights alone. "You could've had plenty of company, if you'd have wanted it. Especially that guy seated at the bar who was willing to pay for your drinks all night."

She clicked her tongue. "I'd never accept an offer like that. And I'd hoped you hadn't heard any of that background noise."

Nate had actually heard plenty, enough to wish he'd been there in person that night. Would she have accepted his offer to buy her drinks?

"Okay," she said. "I'd really like to forget about my fifteen minutes at that cowboy bar. Can't you let it go?"

For now, he supposed. But the subject would undoubtedly come up again. He was having too much fun with it.

"So," Anna said, apparently deciding to change topics for him. "How are things going with the baby?"

"Okay, I guess." He was still a little nervous when he had her on his own, but he was getting the hang of changing diapers and giving her bottles. He could actually get a burp out of her now. And just the other day, he could have sworn she'd smiled at him, but one of the oldsters insisted she just had gas.

"Then I assume you're adjusting to fatherhood."

Nate sure hoped so. He stole another glance at the attractive social worker. She didn't seem to be in any rush to return to the house—or to leave the ranch altogether.

Did she spend this much time with all of her clients? Hell, just the drive to and from the Rocking C had to take more than an hour out of her day. Surely he wasn't her only assignment, the only one she'd taken under her wing—or placed on her radar.

"How many babies and families are you working with?" he asked.

"About seven right now."

That was a lot more than he'd thought, which was a huge relief. At least he wasn't her only focus.

Still, if each of those parents got as much of her time and attention as he did, she must really be busy—not to mention dedicated. He admired that about her. And for that very reason, he could see why it bothered her when he teased her about throwing down a couple of drinks and kicking up her heels.

"Do you live near the Stagecoach Inn?" he asked.

"Oh, no. I'm on the other side of town, near the hospital. I rent a studio apartment, but after that pipe broke the other day, there was so much water damage I had to move out temporarily."

"You mentioned that you had to stay at the Night Owl. Were you able to find another place to stay?"

"Actually, I'm still there."

He blew out a long, slow whistle. "Something tells me that's a far cry from what you're used to."

Anna laughed, and as she let down her guard, her shoulder brushed his arm in a casual, we're-becoming-friends way. "You're right about that. I'd much rather be at the Four Seasons or the Ritz, but that wasn't an option in Brighton Valley—or even in Wexler."

He'd pretty much pegged her as a five-star hotel gal, so it appeared that he'd gotten that part right.

"I hate living out of a suitcase," she said. "And unfortunately, the construction work is going to take a lot longer than anyone expected. So, as much as I like my cozy little apartment, especially since it's walking distance to the hospital, I'm going to take a couple of days off work so I can find another place to live."

"While you're looking, there's a new condominium complex near my house. It's located fairly close to the hospital, too. You might want to check it out."

"The condos on the corner of Oakdale and Peachtree Lane? I've seen them. They look nice, but I can't afford to buy anything right now. And to make matters worse, my place is completely furnished. So I'd have to invest in..." She paused then gave a slight shrug. "Well, furniture and pretty much everything else. So needless to say, some of my time off will be spent shopping for home furnishings."

She had no furniture of her own, no household stuff? He hadn't seen that coming.

Nate glanced out at the darkened ranch, unsure of which direction to go next. But for the time being, as long as Anna was walking by his side, he didn't really care where they went.

Anna Reynolds was proving to be a surprising woman. And one who could easily intrigue him to distraction.

Anna had no idea why she and Nate had wandered nearly a hundred yards from the ranch house. The excuse she'd given him, as well as herself, was to talk privately so she could check on how the new daddy was doing with his daughter. But it seemed that their conversation had been more about her and her living situation. As a result, this evening's home visit was beginning to turn into something she hadn't meant it to be.

What had she been thinking?

That was the problem. She hadn't been thinking. She'd been too caught up in the moment, in the intimacy of walking with a handsome man in the moonlight. And she was supposed to be working.

She stole a peek at Nate, who sauntered beside her as if their nighttime stroll wasn't anything out of the ordinary. But it was.

Did he assume she only wanted to get him alone so she could get to know him better on a personal level?

Okay, so maybe there was some of that going on. She was more than a little curious about Nate. She wanted to know more about him—and as a man and not just a daddy. And for that reason it was time to contain her wayward thoughts.

She slowed to a stop. "I almost forgot. The main reason I drove out here was to tell you I'd gotten the information you'd wanted. I have the name of the woman who manages that company that provides trained and bonded nannies."

"Oh, good."

"Yes, but I left it in my briefcase. We'd better head back to the house so I can get it for you."

"Okay." Nate continued to walk along a path that seemed to lead to nowhere in particular.

"I also need to get home before it gets much later," she added. And before she completely lost her head about why she was really here.

Nate stopped and turned to face her. As his gaze snagged hers, his smile went from boyish and teasing to one that was almost flirtatious. "That's a bad sign, Anna."

"What is?" She tilted her head slightly, trying to read his expression. She had no idea what he thought was a "bad" sign.

"You referred to the Night Owl as home."

Oh, gosh. She had, but she hadn't meant it that way. She'd only wanted to get away from here, from him, before she said or implied too much.

"Don't worry," she said. "I haven't begun to nest there. I'm just ready to turn in for the night, and that motel is the closest thing I have to a home these days."

He studied her with an intensity she hadn't expected or been ready for. Her heart spun in her chest, and her breathing slowed to a near standstill. She was so mesmerized by it all—the way he was looking at her, the effect he had on her—that she couldn't seem to move at all.

She both wanted and needed to escape whatever was going on between them, but she was drawn to it, ensnared by it.

This was so not good. She had to shake it off, to gather her thoughts and rely on her common sense.

"That's why I need to start looking for a new place," she said. "And why I want to get home… I mean *back* to the motel before it gets much later."

"Then I'll walk you to your car."

An audible response stalled in her throat, so all she could do was nod and turn toward the front yard, avoiding the longer graveled path and taking a short cut across the lawn instead.

Nate didn't say anything, either, and she was glad about that. Yet they'd seemed to be communicating silently, although she'd be darned if she knew what that was all about.

Okay, so she suspected she knew what it might be, what it could be, but she refused to put any more weight on the pounding of her heart, the flutter in her belly.

As they neared the barn, the motion detector picked up their movements, and the outdoor lights came on. But before she could head toward the house to get her purse and briefcase, an engine sounded. She glanced at the driveway and spotted the oncoming headlights of a vehicle heading to the ranch.

A pickup, she suspected. A black one that appeared to be shiny and new.

"Well, I'll be damned," Nate said.

"Who is it?"

"Drew Madison."

The name sounded familiar, but Anna couldn't put her finger on why it would.

As the man—a rather tall one in his mid- to late-thirties—climbed from his truck, Anna took a good look at him, trying to recognize him to no avail.

He wore a dark cowboy hat, but under it, his longish hair appeared to be light brown—maybe even blond. He had broad shoulders and was ruggedly built.

Still, Anna didn't recognize him. Should she?

The man—Drew—strode toward Nate with his arm outstretched in greeting. "Hey, how's it going, buddy?"

Nate shook his hand. "I'm doin' all right."

The handsome, well-dressed cowboy glanced at Anna and smiled. Then he doffed his hat. "How'd you do, ma'am? I'm Andrew Madison, but you can call me Drew."

He was nearly as handsome as Nate, and his manners were certainly admirable. There was something likable about the guy, but she still had no idea why his name sounded familiar.

She reached out and took his hand. "Anna Reynolds. It's nice to meet you."

His grip was warm and firm as he flashed a dimpled grin.

Anna glanced at Nate, only to see that he wasn't returning the man's smile.

So who was Drew Madison? And why didn't Nate seem to be as happy to see him as he was to see Nate?

When Nate had spotted Drew climbing out of a new truck, his steps had slowed to a stop. It wasn't unusual for Drew to drop by the Rocking C, but whenever he did, it made Nate a little uneasy.

Not that Nate had anything against the guy. In fact, he liked him. They'd been good friends in high school, and for a while they'd been competitors. Actually, they still were. Friends, that is. But they no longer had the rodeo in common.

And that was the problem. Seeing Drew only

served to remind Nate of the life he no longer had—and the man he no longer was.

Of course, that wasn't Drew's fault. It really wasn't anyone's. Out of the blue, life struck a mean blow, and a man learned to roll with the punches. Unfortunately, it seemed that Nate had been rolling with the unexpected for as long as he could remember, and he was getting tired of it. The punches, that is.

"I stopped by to see Rex," Drew said.

Nate motioned toward the house. "He's inside."

"I didn't mean to—" Drew didn't exactly wink at Nate, but he may as well have "—interrupt anything."

"You didn't."

Drew's lips quirked into a crooked grin, suggesting he had his doubts. But whether he believed it or not, there wasn't anything romantic going on between Nate and Anna.

Or was there?

Nate stole a peek at the pretty social worker and, noting the quizzical expression on her face, figured an explanation was in order.

"When we were younger, Drew and I once competed in the rodeo," Nate said. "But then he went off to college."

Anna smiled warmly at the cowboy. A little too warmly, if you asked Nate, since Drew, with his sandy blond hair, blue eyes and dimpled grin, was what you'd call a real ladies' man. The guy had a way of charming a good girl to be naughty.

"It's nice to meet you," Anna said. "But I was just leaving, so you'll have to excuse me." She turned back to Nate and nodded toward the house. "I need to get my purse and briefcase. I also have that referral I told you about."

"Thanks," Nate said. "I appreciate that."

As Anna headed toward the front porch steps, Drew eased closer to Nate and lowered his voice to a whisper. "Looks like you're moving up these days."

From what? The women who'd thrown themselves at his feet until his career ended?

"Anna's a social worker from the hospital," Nate said. "She comes to check on Beth's baby."

"You mean *your* baby?"

One night, after having a couple of beers, Nate had told Drew about his brief relationship with Beth.

"You're right. She's mine. Being a father takes a little getting used to."

"I can only imagine." Drew glanced at the house, where the screen door had just clicked shut. "I'll bet it also puts a cramp in your social life."

Nate wondered if Drew's social life had also slowed down, after he'd given up the rodeo himself. But Drew hadn't suffered a career-ending injury. He'd inherited his family's ranch after his uncle J.P. passed away and was taking his new responsibilities seriously.

After J. P. Madison died last winter, Drew had remained in contact with J.P.'s friend, Rex Mayberry, who lived on the Rocking Chair Ranch. Rex had asked Drew to find a sponsor for the retired cowboys' home, and Drew had agreed to help by using his rodeo connections.

Nate had those same connections once upon a time, but he'd more or less broken away from them so he wouldn't have the constant reminder of the life he'd once had.

"I was sorry to hear about Beth," Drew said. "She was a real sweetheart and didn't deserve what that brute did to her."

"Yeah, I know. But Kenny told her he was sorry for hitting her in the past and swore he'd never do it again. And unfortunately, Beth believed him."

Drew tilted up the brim of his Stetson. "Guys like Kenny Huddleston don't change."

"I tried to tell her that, but she… Well, Beth was convinced that he'd turned over a new leaf. At least he's in jail for what he did."

"To tell you the truth, I was surprised to hear that you stepped up and took custody of the baby. I assume you had a DNA test."

Nate had told Drew about Beth's claim, about the possibility that he might have fathered her baby. But he hadn't shared his doubts. "I don't need a blood test," he said.

"You're *that* sure?"

Sure enough to know that he hadn't wanted the baby to go to foster care—or to any of Kenny's relatives. "Yep. There's no question that Jessie's my daughter."

"Well, I admire you. Being a single dad can't be easy."

It sure as hell wasn't, but before Nate could respond, the front door squeaked open and Sam walked out of the house and into the porch light. "Well, I'll be damned. Look what the cat dragged in." Sam crossed the yard to join them and greeted Drew with a warm, friendly handshake. "It's always good to see you, son."

"I hear congratulations are in order," Drew said. "Rex told me there's a wedding on the horizon."

"That's right." The sparkle in Sam's eye could have lit the entire yard, and he grinned from ear to ear. "Joy and I are getting married next month."

Nate wasn't exactly surprised to hear that news since it was no secret the older couple was head over heels for each other, but he hadn't realized the plans were underway. "You've already set a date?"

"We just decided today," Sam said. "I was going to talk to you about it tomorrow morning. I want you to take over my ranch duties while I'm on my honeymoon. We're going to Hawaii for a couple of weeks, then on to New Zealand."

Talk about extended trips. "How long will you be gone?" Nate asked.

"A long, long time, if I have anything to say about it." Sam chuckled. "Surely you aren't worried that you can't handle things around here without me."

"No, not at all. It's just that..." Well, Nate hadn't planned to be a permanent ranch hand or even a foreman on someone else's spread. His job on the Rocking C was only meant to be a temporary gig until he figured out what he wanted to do with the rest of his life. "I just wondered how long you'd be gone."

"Four weeks or longer," Sam said. "But don't

worry. I can't think of a more competent man to take over for me."

"I second that." Drew tossed a grin at Nate. "The Rocking C will be in good hands." Then he returned his attention to Sam. "So when's the happy event going to take place?"

"The fifteenth of next month. We'll have the ceremony here, followed by a big reception. Joy's already making arrangements to have it catered since I'm not going to let my bride get stuck in the kitchen on her wedding day."

"You'll need to find a good replacement for Joy, too," Nate told Sam. "Otherwise, I predict a big revolt while you're gone. She's got these men spoiled with her cooking and TLC."

Sam laughed. "Ain't that the truth? But don't worry. We'll find someone who can put together a tasty meal."

Before Nate could respond, the door squeaked open again. This time Anna exited the house, the long strap of her purse draped over her shoulder. She held a brochure in one hand and her briefcase in the other.

Nate shot a glance at Drew, only to see him zeroing in on Anna. It grated him to know she'd caught the other man's interest, but he really couldn't blame Drew. Anna was a tempting sight to behold.

When Nate returned his gaze to Anna, she was wearing a breezy smile aimed at him, one that filled his chest with warmth.

"Here's that information I told you about." She

handed him the brochure. "If you have any questions after looking this over, give me a call."

But only call her if he had questions?

Shake it off, Gallagher. Anna Reynolds isn't interested in cowboys.

But then again, her focus shifted to Drew, and she seemed to be checking him out right now. Maybe she was just curious about him and why he'd come this evening.

Apparently, so was Sam. "Is there any news on that rodeo sponsorship?" the foreman asked.

"As a matter of fact, there is. And it's good news, too. Ramon Esteban, the head of the rodeo, likes the idea of sponsoring the Rocking Chair Ranch. He also wants to meet whoever's in charge and take a tour of the place. That's why I drove out here tonight. I wanted to tell Rex in person."

"That's great," Sam said. "Let's go inside. I can't wait to hear what Rex has to say about it."

Drew slapped his hand on the older man's back, then the two headed for the ranch house, leaving Nate and Anna alone. As their eyes met, that flood of warmth returned to Nate's chest, and every nerve ending he had snapped to attention.

Neither of them spoke or made a move for what seemed like forever, but was probably only a minute.

Finally, when the floodlights dimmed, Anna nodded toward her car. "I'd better go. Not *home*, but to bed."

Nate's thoughts drifted to a bedroom setting, to

soft lighting, romantic music playing in the background, satin sheets turned down…

He slowly shook his head, trying to dislodge the image. There was no way he'd consider sleeping with the social worker assigned to his case. He had to get his mind back to reality.

"Good night," Anna said. Then she walked to her car. As she climbed behind the wheel and started the engine, Nate had half a notion to call her back, to…

To do what? Ask her to go out with him?

No way. But as she drove away, he had second thoughts.

Why the hell not?

Chapter Six

Something had happened to Anna at the Rocking C last night, although she wasn't entirely sure just what it was. She'd experienced an awakening of some kind, a growing awareness of something she hadn't realized before, and it had drawn her to Nate in a different way.

She had to admit that there was also something about him that stirred her hormones. Under normal circumstances, that swirl of heat and desire should have bothered her, but for some reason it didn't. Maybe that was because there was more than just sexual attraction at play.

She'd seen something flicker in his eyes, although just briefly. She'd sensed that he had an invisible wound of some kind, one he tried to hide with humor. Drew's unexpected arrival had sparked that look again, revealing a tiny crack in Nate's armor and further convincing Anna that there was much more to him than she'd realized. And, as a result, she found herself thinking about him all that night and into the next morning.

Since it was now officially the weekend and she didn't have to work, she ate breakfast at Caroline's Diner. Then she crossed the street to Nettles Realty. Before going in, she stood outside the office and checked out the photos of homes and ranches displayed on the front window.

Several properties looked appealing, especially a small white house with a picket fence, a pretty yard and a red front door. But ever since Anna had landed the job at the medical center, she'd been making double payments on her student loans. That had seemed to be a good idea at the time, but her effort to get out of debt quickly had limited the amount she'd been able to put into savings.

Like she'd told Nate, she wasn't in a position to purchase anything right now, but maybe Mr. Nettles had a list of rentals available. So she opened the glass door and entered the small, cluttered office.

An older man who appeared to be past the retirement age looked up from his desk, pushed aside the crossword puzzle he'd been working on and smiled. "Hello, there."

"Mr. Nettles?" she asked.

"Yes, but call me Ralph. How can I help you?"

Maybe coming inside hadn't been a good idea after

all. Anna tucked a strand of hair behind her ear then clutched the shoulder strap of her purse. "I…uh… don't suppose you know of any homes or apartments for rent in the downtown area."

"Sorry. I'm afraid not. I do have a few options if you're in the market to buy."

"Not unless you're aware of anything that wouldn't require a large down payment."

Ralph stroked his chin, giving that some thought, then slowly shook his head. "No, not really, although there's a property on Briar Patch that might become available soon. The woman who owned it passed away unexpectedly, and her only heir is a surgeon who lives out of state. From what I understand, there isn't a mortgage or a lien against it, so the new owner might be willing to work with a qualified buyer."

Other than having very little to put down, a student loan and a modest car payment, Anna considered herself "qualified." At least she had a good job.

"Do you think he would accept a small amount down?" she asked.

"He might. The yard hasn't been kept up in years. And the woman was a bit of a hoarder. The doctor would have to hire a landscaper, a cleaning crew and probably a handyman to fix it up before I can actually list it for sale. So he might be willing to let you trade your labor as part of the down payment, just so he didn't have to fly to Texas and deal with it."

Anna wasn't afraid of hard work, but she needed a place she could move into *now*. And that particular house sounded like a rat trap. She'd probably be better off staying at the Night Owl. At least it was clean.

"As soon as I get a key," Mr. Nettles said, "I'd be happy to show it to you."

She supposed it wouldn't hurt to take a look at it, so she said, "All right." Then she reached into her purse, withdrew a business card and a pen. After jotting down her cell phone number on the back, she handed it to the Realtor. "Here's my contact information."

"You know, the more I think about it, that house on Briar Patch might work out to be a good deal for both you and the doctor."

"If you get a key or can show me some photos," she said, "let me know. It sounds like something I might want to consider."

But she probably wouldn't consider it very long. If the owner didn't want to tackle the necessary cleanup and repairs, her studio apartment might be finished long before the house on Briar Patch was habitable.

As she turned to go, she spotted a bulletin board on the wall near the door that had a couple of flyers tacked on it. She assumed they advertised other homes for sale, but when she noticed one announcing a church bazaar, as well as one for a car rally in Wexler, she took a moment to read up on the various community events. She really needed to get out more and meet some of her neighbors.

Her eye was drawn to a red, white and blue poster that displayed Nate Gallagher's name and picture, noting that he was a local boy and a champion. So she studied it closely, particularly the photo of the handsome cowboy, his hat tilted just right, a grin that boasted both skill and pride.

"That rodeo is already past," Ralph said. "I just keep that poster displayed because that bronc rider happens to be the grandson of my old friend, Clinton McClain—God rest his soul."

"You knew Nate's grandfather?" she asked.

"Yep. Clint was a champion bareback rider and all-round rodeo cowboy. After he retired from the circuit, he bought a ranch. A couple of years ago he asked me to list it for him. When it sold, he and his wife bought a place in town."

She thought about that first day she arrived on the Rocking C and saw Nate gentling that gelding. Apparently, he'd learned his skill from his grandfather.

"When Nate moved to the Double M," Ralph said, "he was half grown, but he took to riding and roping like he'd been born in a saddle. He had more talent than most and promised to be a better cowboy than his granddad. That is, until he got busted up by a bronc named Fire in the Hole. Doctors said he was lucky to be alive, but he had to give up riding and find a safer line of work."

"That must have been disappointing," she said. Was that the pain she'd spotted in his eyes Monday night? Had seeing Drew reminded him of all he'd lost?

"To make matters worse," Ralph added, "while Nate was recovering in the hospital, Clint and his wife were killed in a car accident on their way to visit him."

Anna's heart crumpled. "I'm sorry to hear that."

"Yep. It was a real shame, too. Because from what I'd heard, Nate's dad had been a real loser and probably drank himself to death after abandoning the poor kid in foster care. When Clint learned where Nate had ended up, he took custody and brought him to live at the Double M."

Anna hardly had a moment to consider how all of that might have affected Nate when the telephone rang.

"Excuse me, but I have to get this," Ralph said as he reached across the desk for the receiver and answered. "Nettles Realty. This is Ralph."

Anna decided to slip out the door while he was talking. Once outside, she pondered her options for spending the rest of her day. She could drive to Wexler and go shopping, but that would mean spending money she'd rather hold on to until she could find a better housing situation. She could also hang out in the library, which was far more appealing than going back to her dinky hotel room and watching television. Then another idea came to mind.

She could drive out to the Rocking C to visit Nate again.

Oh, for Pete's sake.

He might think that she had romantic thoughts about him, which was the last thing in the world she wanted him to suspect.

Especially since she feared that was true.

* * *

Ever since Anna left the ranch last night, something had been nagging at Nate, prompting him to give her a call. He had an idea, an offer to make, and he didn't want to wait to mention it until she got around to visiting him again.

So after he finished his chores, he asked Joy and Sam to watch Jessie for him. Then he took a shower and headed to town.

He wasn't entirely sure what he'd do if he arrived at the Night Owl Motel and didn't find Anna there. He supposed he could swing by the Stagecoach Inn, have a beer and listen to music for a while. After all, he had a babysitter, and it was the first time he'd lined up something like that when he wasn't actually working.

It felt a little weird to leave Jessie for the evening, but Sam and Joy seemed eager to have her, and Nate knew she'd be in good hands.

By the time he arrived at the motel, it was nearly six o'clock. A few miles back he began to think he should have called Anna first. Even when he spotted her car parked in front of room ten, he considered reaching for his cell phone.

Instead, after parking in a nearby space, he made his way to the door of the room he assumed was hers. A hum of voices sounded from within, and he guessed that she was watching television. He hesitated only a moment before lifting his hand and giving it two solid knocks.

"Who is it?" Anna called out.

"It's Nate."

When she swung open the door, he nearly laughed at her stunned expression, as well as her appearance. Her long, blond hair was slightly mussed, and she wasn't wearing any makeup. She had on an oversize T-shirt and a pair of faded blue jeans. Her bare feet bore a pretty shade of pink toenail polish.

She clearly hadn't expected company tonight and fidgeted in the doorway. She fiddled with her hair as if trying to comb out the tangles with her fingers. But damn, she looked good just as she was.

"Are you up for dinner?" he asked.

Her brow furrowed and her head tilted slightly. Apparently, the question surprised her even more than his arrival had.

"I thought you might want me to chase off any cowboys or truckers who might try to put the moves on you."

Her gaze shot toward the café at the end of the parking lot then to the bar across the busy highway. "You want to eat *here*?"

"Only if you want to. If you like Chinese food, there's a restaurant about ten minutes from here called the Green Dragon." His lips curled into a boyish grin. "They even serve wine—if you feel the need to unwind again."

Again, she fingered her hair then tugged at the gray shirt she was wearing.

"But if you'd rather," he said, "we can walk across the street and have one of those juicy burgers."

"Actually, Chinese sounds good to me. And I'd

love an excuse to get out of here. But I'll need to change clothes and freshen up first."

"You look great just the way you are." And she did.

"Get out of here. I'm a real mess."

His grin deepened. "Just for the record, I think you wear laid-back and casual well."

"Thanks, but I feel frumpy." She stepped aside and let him into the room. "Just give me a few minutes to change and fix my hair."

It actually took her more than a few minutes, although he didn't mind. And when she came out of the bathroom, it had been worth the wait.

She wore a pair of snug black jeans and a cream-colored sweater that revealed her womanly curves. He'd always suspected that she had a dynamite body, but his vivid, masculine imagination hadn't done her shapely figure justice. He wasn't about to admit it, but she wore sexy well, too.

"Shall we go?" he asked.

She nodded then snatched her purse and the room key from the nightstand. Before long they were in his pickup and on the road.

"Apparently, you haven't been able to move home yet," Nate said as he drove toward Main Street. "Do you have any idea when the repair work will be done?"

"No, I don't. It looks like my temporary displacement is turning into a long-term situation. They found mold in the walls so they called a hazardous waste company to remove it and haul it away. They also tore up the foundation to get to the leak. Before they could reroute the plumbing overhead and replace the concrete and flooring, the guy who owns the construction company had a death in the family…" She blew out a weary sigh. "I feel bad for him, but it looks like I'm stuck at the Night Owl for the time being. I'm not sure how much longer I can handle living in a small motel room, so I'm checking into alternatives."

"Living out of a suitcase can be a pain."

"Tell me about it."

Nate glanced across the seat at Anna. Worry marred her brow, and she was biting down on her bottom lip.

"You know," he said, "I have a place in town that I'm not using. You're welcome to stay there, if you want to."

She turned to him, eyes wide and lips parted. "That's a nice offer, but I don't think it's a good idea."

"Why not? It's not only vacant, but it's completely furnished."

She didn't respond right away, but she seemed to be pondering the idea. Or else she was trying to come up with an excuse to decline.

"It's also within walking distance to the hospital," he added, "although it's a bit of a hike. And it's close to Caroline's Diner and all those shops on Main Street."

"It does sound tempting."

He hoped he wouldn't be sorry for offering to let her stay at his place, but he couldn't think of a reason why he would be.

Moments later he pointed out the entrance to the

Green Dragon. When they reached the white building with the red-and-black trim, he turned into the parking lot and found a space in back. Then they got out of his pickup and walked to the front entrance.

"It was nice of you to suggest dinner," Anna said.

"My pleasure." He opened the black door for her and waited for her to enter.

As Anna looked around, taking in the Chinese-style decor and the wallpaper with green dragons splattered on a white background, a red-haired waitress approached the front desk and greeted them. Her auburn locks had been swept up in a prim bun held together by a pair of fancy chopsticks.

"Two for dinner?" she asked.

When Nate told her yes, she grabbed a couple of menus and escorted them past several families and an older couple, stopping at a booth in the back of the restaurant. "Will this be all right?"

"It's fine. Thanks." Nate waited for Anna to slip in and then took his seat.

"Can I get you a drink?" the redhead asked. "Or maybe a pot of tea?"

"I'll have a beer." Nate looked at Anna. "Did you want a glass of wine?"

She thought about it a moment then gave a slight shrug. "Sure. Why not?"

The waitress nodded, handed over the menus and slipped off to get their drinks.

"You came at the perfect time," Anna said. "I was getting hungry, and I wasn't in the mood for burgers and fries."

"Actually, the Stagecoach Inn has a pretty large menu selection. You could have ordered soup, salad or even grilled salmon or prime rib."

"I don't like rowdy crowds, so this is a lot more appealing to me. Plus, I haven't had Chinese food in a long time."

"Then I'm glad it worked out."

When the waitress returned with their drinks, Nate lifted his beer in a toast, just as he'd once imagined doing—only he hadn't envisioned the green dragon wallpaper in the background.

Taking the hint, Anna clinked her wineglass against his bottle.

"Tell me something," she said.

Uh-oh. What did she want to know? The uneasiness he'd once felt whenever he talked to her in the past settled over him again.

"You mentioned that you were injured when riding in the rodeo," she said. "And that you had to give it up."

He shrugged as if none of it had really mattered, when it had. And more than most people would know. For years, Nate had been trying to prove himself, first to his old man then later to his grandfather. And just as he'd finally done it—made something out of his life—he'd crashed and burned, thanks to Fire in the Hole. Then, to make matters worse, he lost Grandpa Clint before he could come up with a plan B.

"Having a career-ending injury must have been tough," Anna said.

"It was, but I'm dealing with it."

Anna didn't know it, but Nate had suffered a lot of disappointing events in his life, starting with his mother's death when he was only in kindergarten. But he'd learned to handle each one that came his way.

"I imagine that giving up the rodeo is something you're going to be 'dealing with' for quite a while."

She was right, but he shrugged it off. "I can still walk—and work." Even if he only meant for that job at the Rocking C to be short-term.

He nearly chuffed at the irony. Just like Anna's temporary stay at the Night Owl had started out.

She took a sip of wine, her eyes lingering on him. "You seem to be very good with horses. I saw you working with one the first day I arrived."

Some people considered it a gift, but Nate didn't want to boast, so he thanked her for the compliment.

"You obviously have a gift," she said.

"My grandfather owned a ranch, and when I was in middle school, he managed to track me down..." He paused. That was way too much information for a woman who seemed to be too damned curious about him and his past.

"You mean, he found you? Where?"

See? He'd stepped right into that one. Again he shrugged. "I was living with a foster family at the time. My grandfather hadn't seen my mom in years and didn't even know he had a grandson. So when he found out about her death and my existence, he took me to live with him on his ranch."

"So that's where you learned about horses. That's impressive."

"My grandfather was a retired rodeo champ, and I thought that was pretty cool. So I decided to be just like him when I grew up."

"I heard you became a champion in your own right."

That was true. He'd actually had a few happy and lucrative years. But he wasn't sure where she'd heard about that. "Who've you been talking to?"

"Ralph Nettles. He said you might've been a better cowboy than your grandfather."

Nate had certainly tried to be. Grandpa Clint had been a stranger to him for the first thirteen years of his life, but then he'd taught Nate everything there was to know about being a cowboy. He also taught him that a man who was worth his salt owned up to his mistakes and took responsibility for his kin.

"I hope he was proud of me," Nate said, "but I guess I'll never know for sure."

Anna smiled, her eyes glistening as if Nate had somehow made her proud, too. But how could she be when she didn't even know him—or the man he used to be?

"I'm sorry about that accident," she said. "But I'm glad you're making the best of it."

Was he? He was certainly trying to.

Even though he didn't like talking about it, for some reason, it seemed okay to share his reality with Anna this evening.

"After I was thrown and trampled, the orthopedic surgeon managed to put me back together, but he said

I needed to choose another career, one that wasn't as dangerous." Nate lifted his beer. "So here I am."

"Working on a ranch doesn't seem all that safe to me," she said.

"I could get banged up anywhere. Besides, I'm feeling pretty good these days. I might even try riding a bronc again."

"But you could get hurt."

"I'm not afraid of that." He was more afraid of getting back in the saddle and learning that the doctor had been right. That he no longer had what it took to hold on and ride those eight seconds. "But just for the record, I'm grateful to be alive—and walking on my own two feet."

Nate might be downplaying it all, especially when talking to Anna, but that near-fatal injury and lengthy hospitalization had brought about a real reckoning for him on many levels. He'd once been happy-go-lucky and had his choice of ladies, but his life was a lot quieter these days. And he was much more introspective.

Giving up his dream had been a tough row to hoe. And he was still trying to figure out what to do with the changes he'd had to make—and not just in terms of his career.

But if Anna thought she was wearing him down and that he was going to get all soft and share his innermost feelings, she was wrong.

"Have you thought about my offer?" he asked, steering the conversation away from his accident. "Do you want to move into my house?"

As if dragging her feet and pondering an answer,

she lifted her glass and took a sip of wine. Finally, she said, "To be honest, I'm tired of living in a motel. So yes, if you don't mind, I'd like to take you up on your kindness and generosity."

"Good. I'll give you a key and you can move in as soon as tomorrow." He tossed her one of his happy-go-lucky smiles, although it didn't feel especially lighthearted or sincere.

But he'd made the offer and would follow through on it. He just hoped that, in the long run, he didn't regret it.

Anna couldn't believe she'd agreed to move into Nate's house, but on the other hand, she couldn't wait to check out of the Night Owl, so she wasn't going to stress about it.

First thing the next morning she followed the directions he'd given her and drove to 331 Peachtree Lane, a quaint and quiet neighborhood. To say that she was surprised to see where she would be temporarily staying was an understatement. She'd never expected Nate to have such a nice place to live. In fact, if his truck hadn't been parked in the driveway of the pale green, two-story house, she would have taken a second look at the address he'd written down for her and checked it against the numbers on the white fascia trim.

Did rodeo cowboys make that kind of money? She doubted that ranch hands did. But then again, did it really matter? It had been kind of him to offer to let her stay here.

After parking along the curb, she left her bags in the trunk and made her way to the front door, all the while checking out the newly mowed lawn, the manicured bushes and colorful flower beds. He must have a gardener. How else could he keep things looking so green and maintained?

Nate had given her a key last night, but she didn't want to use it if he was home. So she rang the bell instead and waited for him to answer.

When the door swung open, the sight of him, with his hair damp from the shower, darn near took her breath away.

"Good. You're here." As he stepped aside to let her in, she walked past him and caught the scent of soap and musk.

She shook off the compulsion to take a second, lingering whiff of the man and focused on the living room instead, with its hardwood floor, brown leather furniture and brightly colored Southwestern artwork on the walls.

A built-in bookshelf next to a stone fireplace was filled with a variety of novels, all hardbound. It was impressive. When did he have time to read?

She wasn't sure what she'd been expecting, but certainly not a warm and cozy place like this, and couldn't help asking, "Do you live alone?"

"Yes, although I've been known to have a few sleepovers."

She shot a glance at him, watched a grin stretch across his face. Was he implying that he dated a lot of women?

Of course he was. And it really wasn't any of her business if he did, although she figured the decor might have had a woman's touch.

"Your home is beautiful," she said as she continued her perusal. "I really like the paintings."

"My grandfather's wife was an artist," he said.

A step-grandmother? Anna didn't give that too much thought. After all, divorces were fairly common. She continued to study the interior. From what she could see, it was clean and tidy. Did he have a housekeeper?

If anything, her curiosity about the handsome cowboy was growing by leaps and bounds. And in spite of the constant self-reminders that it wasn't her concern, she wanted to know more about him. A lot more.

"Where are your things?" Nate asked. "You didn't change your mind about staying here, did you?"

"I left them in the car. I was going to get my bags later." After she'd talked to him. After she'd made sure she really wanted to stay.

But why wouldn't she? The house was only about a mile from the hospital. It was also going to be a nice place to come home to after a trying day at work.

"I'll show you around," Nate said. Then he proceeded to do just that, starting with a well-stocked kitchen that had stainless-steel appliances and a granite countertop.

"I picked up a few things at the grocery store," he said. "Milk, eggs, bread and that sort of thing. I thought you'd be able to get by with that until you were able to go shopping yourself."

"You didn't need to go to that much trouble."

He shrugged a single shoulder. "I know, but I figured you'd want to get settled."

So he was not only generous, but thoughtful, too.

After he showed her the laundry room, they headed upstairs and then down the hallway. He stopped at the first open door. "This is the guest room. I think you'll be comfortable sleeping here. And you'll have a private bathroom."

The room was twice as big as the one she'd had at the Night Owl and larger than the one she had at the studio apartment. "This is perfect, Nate. I really appreciate you letting me stay here. Just let me know how much rent you'd like."

He waved her off. "I don't want a dime. And you can stay as long as you like." Then he continued the tour, pointing out the linen closet, as well as his master suite—something decidedly masculine with bold, dark furniture and a green comforter draped over a king-size, four-poster bed.

Even though he hadn't been sleeping there, she still caught the remnant of his woodsy cologne.

"Oh," he said as he led her out to the hallway. "You'll probably want to see this." Then he pointed out a smaller room opposite his. It appeared to have been an art studio. His step-grandmother's?

"I thought I'd make this room into a nursery for Jessie," he said.

"Good idea. It's just the right size, and it should be fun to decorate."

He chuckled. "I don't know about that. I have no

clue what she's going to need. So I'll have to ask the new nanny to help me."

"You hired someone already?"

"No, not yet. But I'll ask for her help when it's time."

Time for what? For him to stop relying on the women at the ranch? Wasn't he the least bit eager to bring the baby home to stay?

Maybe Anna would have to do something to help move things along. The sooner he and his daughter got settled into his own house, the better.

"I have some vacation hours built up," she said. "I was going to use some of it to look for a place to rent. But I can also use the time to help you find a nanny. It shouldn't take us too long to find someone you can trust."

He seemed to stew on that suggestion a while. A long while.

She'd suspected that he might have grown too dependent upon Joy and the nurses for childcare, and that worried her. Bonding was so important in the early weeks and months. So she threw out another idea.

"Why don't you bring Jessie home now? I can watch her while you're at work for a week or two. And that would give you time to hire someone else."

Had she really made that suggestion? It had seemed like the right thing to do at the time, but what if he took her up on it?

And what if he wasn't happy with any of the nannies they interviewed? Was she actually willing to babysit for him until he found a replacement? Maybe she should backpedal on her suggestion, although she wasn't entirely sure how to pull that off gracefully.

So she opened her mouth, ready to admit that her idea might not be the best solution after all, but before she could utter a word, the handsome cowboy nodded his head, agreeing to her crazy proposal.

Chapter Seven

Nate hadn't expected Anna to offer to help him move back to his house with Jessie, and he'd tried to think of a good reason to decline. But the more he thought about it, the better he liked the idea.

Even though Joy and the nurses were far more capable of taking care of Jessie than he was, it wasn't fair to expect them to look after a baby during the day in addition to their many other responsibilities. Besides, he couldn't continue to stay at the Rocking C indefinitely—and he really didn't want to. He missed his house in town and the comfort and privacy it provided.

After the car accident, Grandpa Clint's attorney had contacted Nate while he was still in the hospital and informed him that he'd inherited the entire estate, which had been considerably more than he'd expected it to be. His only regret was that the Double M was no longer a part of it.

He considered it a blessing to be Clint and Audrey's sole heir, but he would have preferred to own the ranch rather than a house in Brighton Valley, several different bank accounts and a significant stock portfolio. He guessed that was the cowboy in him.

Once he was discharged from the hospital, he moved into the house and had been slowly putting his own mark on it. He might not have purchased that particular property himself, but he'd saved up enough of his rodeo earnings to buy something similar.

Still, he liked the place. It was the closest thing to a real home he could ever remember having, and he had to admit that it would be the perfect neighborhood in which to raise Jessie.

On top of that, his back was killing him from sleeping on that damned sofa in the nurse's office at the Rocking C.

"Okay," he told Anna. "If you're sure you don't mind helping me find a nanny and looking after Jessie until I do, then I'll move back home with the baby."

She smiled, although her eyes didn't reflect an enthusiastic response. Maybe she wasn't as pleased by his agreement as he'd expected her to be.

It was just a guess on his part, but she might be having second thoughts about any number of things, like the fact that she wouldn't be using her education and training while acting as a temporary babysitter. She might also be worried about the amount of time it might take him to find the right person to care for Jessie. He certainly was considering that.

"How long do you think it'll take me to find and hire the right nanny?" he asked.

"I'm not sure, but we can't put this plan into play immediately. I'll need to sign off on your case first. I'd also have to double-check with my supervisor about taking most of my vacation time. I have three weeks built up, so that should be enough time to allow me to help you during the transition."

Nate didn't know what to say. He'd already agreed to let her help him, but he wasn't convinced that finding a nanny would be a slam dunk. It wasn't going to be easy letting a complete stranger move into his house and watch the baby while he was at work. What if the woman he hired didn't work out? What if he had to start the selection process all over again?

Worse, what if Anna's three-week vacation wasn't long enough for any complications that could rise up?

"I would only stay during the transition," Anna repeated. "As soon as the new nanny moves in, I'll find another place to live. And once she settles into a routine with the baby, I'll let you get on with your life."

Having Anna around made the whole game plan more feasible, which should make him feel better. But in actuality, that's exactly what worried him. Anna had no idea how afraid he was of failing Jessie, even after she was no longer an infant.

"This is probably going to work out better than you think," Anna said. "It'll help strengthen your father-daughter bond."

Nate had never been worried about that. How could he not love and want to protect that precious little girl? He'd do anything for her—and he'd guard her with his life.

No, that wasn't what scared him.

One night, when Nate had been a teenager, Grandpa Clint had told him, "I probably shouldn't say this, son, but your old man was a real horse's ass. He didn't deserve to have a son like you or a wife like your mom."

As sad as that fact was, Nate had puffed up a bit, taking those words as a compliment. Clint had thought Nate had deserved better.

But then Audrey had added her thoughts. "You make it sound as if Nate's father was a bad seed. But, Clint, the man had a rough life himself and never had a family of his own. How could anyone expect him to be a good husband or father?"

Clint had merely shrugged off her comment, but Audrey had made a good point, and Nate had taken it to heart. And the truth of it still dogged him today.

What if he wasn't able to be a proper parent? Lord knew he'd never had a good role model, other than Clint. But their bond had been slow in coming and was more based upon horsemanship, saddles and lariats. They might have developed a good relationship over time, but it wasn't especially affectionate. In fact, it was more like the bond a rancher had with his favorite cowhand.

If Jessie had been a boy, it might be easier for Nate to do right by her. But what did he know about raising a little girl?

"You seem to be uneasy about something," Anna said. "Are you reconsidering your decision?"

Yes, but he wasn't going to admit why.

"Are *you*?" he asked.

"No, I'm already thinking about what we'll need to do to get that nursery ready. I know you already have a portable crib, which you can use here until you buy a bigger one. But you should get a baby monitor, as well as a few other things. So I might drive to Wexler and pick them up for you."

The thought that he needed anything at all, when he probably needed a ton of things, only reminded him of how much he lacked. And not just in "things."

Still, he thanked her and said, "Get whatever you think Jessie needs, and I'll reimburse you. This house certainly isn't ready for a baby."

"Actually," Anna said, "I think this house is amazing, even as it is. Any child would be happy to grow up here."

That was a huge relief. But would Jessie be happy to have a cowboy for a daddy, a man who didn't know squat about fatherhood or families?

Still, Nate had accepted the responsibility of being Jessie's dad, even if he wasn't entirely sure that he'd fathered her. Hell, he couldn't even think about what might happen to her if she had to live with one of Kenny's shady relatives.

That meant Nate was the best parent she was likely to get. He just hoped he'd never be required to take a DNA test because he was afraid of what the results might reveal.

Grandpa Clint used to say, "The truth will set you free." And that had always made sense to Nate. But when it came to Jessie's paternity, he might be locked into a truth he wasn't ready to face.

As soon as Nate agreed to bring Jessie to live with him at his house, Anna began making a mental list of all the things they'd need to buy and to do before the baby arrived. And as far as she was concerned, they couldn't get started checking off each project or purchase soon enough.

So when Nate reached for the keys to his pickup so he could drive back to the Rocking Chair Ranch for the night, she asked, "Would it be all right if I helped you move things out of the art studio? I can box things up and store them in the garage—or wherever you suggest."

The question seemed to take him aback. Had she pressed him too hard or too soon? Had she stepped over a line?

"Then again," she added, "I just remembered that the room she'll be using once belonged to your grandmother. You probably have keepsakes or family heirlooms in there, so I'm sorry I didn't consider that."

Nate blew out a ragged sigh. "Her name was Audrey. And while she was nice enough to me, we really weren't that close. I doubt there's anything in there that I'd want to keep."

Anna had gathered that he'd suffered a lot of sadness in his life. He'd lost his mother, been abandoned by his father...and now he implied that he hadn't been very close to his grandfather's wife.

Hopefully, creating a new family with Jessie would provide him with some of what he'd missed while growing up.

On the other hand, it was also possible that his past would make it more difficult to bond with his daughter.

"Go ahead and box things up," Nate said. "That is, if you want to. I'll come back tomorrow night and take them out to the shed in the backyard. I can store them in there until I have a chance to go through them. Audrey's sister lives in Pennsylvania. She might be interested in having something as a keepsake."

"That sounds like a good idea to me, especially if they were close."

"They were," Nate said. "She had a heart attack when she got the news about the accident and wasn't able to attend the funeral."

"I'm sorry."

"Yeah, me, too." He picked up his keys then turned toward the door. "Anyway, stuff happens. And life goes on."

Nate seemed to be dealing with all that had happened to him, which was good. He'd probably learned to be adaptable.

Anna certainly had. Life hadn't been easy for her when she was a child, but she'd been a big daydreamer, which had helped her to ignore whatever went on around her and provided her with an imaginary world in which she could escape.

Still, her heart went out to Nate, as well as to the baby girl he was making room for in his home. Hopefully, he was making room for her in his heart. As a social worker, Anna was determined to make sure Jessie grew up in a strong, loving family, even if—God forbid—her father had to live elsewhere.

The next morning Anna drove to a nearby discount store and purchased cardboard boxes in which she could pack up Audrey's art supplies.

Next up was a trip to Babies "R" Us in Wexler so she could pick up a few items Jessie would need. She'd no more than slid behind the wheel and started the ignition when her cell phone rang.

She checked the lighted display. Someone was calling her from the Rocking Chair Ranch, and her heart plummeted to her stomach. Her first thought was that something was wrong, either with Jessie or Nate, and her stomach clenched. She nearly fumbled the phone as she slid her finger across the screen to answer. "Hello?"

"Hey," Joy said, her voice sounding chipper and upbeat. "I hope I'm not bothering you, Anna."

"No, not at all. What's up?"

"Nate told me that you planned to do a little shopping so you could start setting up the nursery, but I wanted to ask you to hold off for a bit."

Anna clutched the phone tighter, and her heart began to speed up again as she realized Nate might be having second thoughts about bringing Jessie home. "Why do you want me to wait?"

"Because we'd like to have a surprise baby shower for Nate. I think we can pull it off by this evening. One of the nurses and an aide volunteered to shop for the men and wrap the gifts. I'll bake a cake this morning and decorate it after lunch. What do you think?"

"I think that's a wonderful idea. How can I help?"

Five minutes later Anna had altered her shopping plans and went to a party store instead, where she stocked up on paper plates, napkins, special favors and a booklet of baby shower games. Next she stopped at a local mall, where she purchased prizes for the winners. She found a candy store and picked up two boxes of chocolate, which she figured anyone would like. She also bought a set of dominoes and a Monopoly game.

She was pleased with all of her purchases, as well as the speed in which she'd done it. Last on her list was a visit to Kiddies' Clothes Corral so she could find the perfect shower gift. Unfortunately, she couldn't seem to zip through the aisles in that store as she'd done in the others.

As she scanned the racks of baby girl clothes, she was tempted to load up on onesies, sleepers and dresses, but she hated to go overboard, no matter how darling some of those little outfits were. Still, she bought one of each.

When she neared the checkout area, she spotted the perfect gift for a little cowgirl—soft denim jeans, a white cotton T-shirt and a pair of tiny pink boots. Jessie might only be nearing six pounds right now, but she would outgrow her few preemie sleepers before Nate realized.

Anna chose the nine-month size then carried an armful of other items to the register.

"Do you have gift boxes and wrapping paper?" she asked the department store clerk.

"I'm afraid not," the woman said. "But we do have tissue, gift bags and a small variety of cards on the rack behind you."

Anna thanked her then chose a bright pink bag, white tissue paper and a frilly bow made of pastel-colored ribbon. Just before handing over her credit card, she spotted a stuffed animal she couldn't resist—a little brown pony.

"Will you add this to my purchase?" she asked.

"You bet."

Her gift totaled more than she'd planned to spend, but she didn't mind. She was happy with all she'd chosen.

Then, with her car loaded down, she drove out to the Rocking C to help Joy create the perfect surprise baby shower for a cowboy daddy.

Nate had spent the afternoon working in the north forty, far from the house. He'd had more work he could have done in the barn, but Sam had insisted he take the Gator out and check the irrigation system.

Now, as he drove back to put away his tools, Sam met him in the yard and nodded toward the barn. "Why don't you clean up in there before coming into the house to eat? Joy invited a few friends to join us for dinner, and I thought it would be easier if the ranch hands didn't use the mudroom as usual."

"Sure." Nate had half a notion to tell him he'd rather return to his own place and eat with Anna, but he figured there'd be some ribbing or comments made about that. Besides, he'd be moving home as soon as the nursery was ready.

He parked the Gator then went into the barn, where he washed his face and hands at the sink in the bathroom. On his way to the house, he spotted a couple of cars, one of which was Anna's.

Why had she come this evening? Was she one of the "friends" Joy had invited to dinner?

His pulse rate soared, although not in apprehension. He was actually looking forward to seeing her again.

Once he reached the front porch, he scraped his boots on the mat then opened the door. He was met with a resounding "Surprise!" followed by hoots and whistles.

What the…hell?

The living room had been draped with pastel-colored streamers, and two long tables had been brought in. One was laden down with food, the other with gifts.

He was still trying to wrap his brain around what was going on when Sam slapped him on the back. "You've got a possum in the headlights look, Nate. Apparently, you've never been to a baby shower before."

He certainly hadn't. He'd never even had a birthday party. Okay, there'd been one, but it hadn't been a big one with friends and decorations and… Dang, this was really something.

Was the celebration for Jessie? It had to be, but everyone, including all the retired cowboys who lived here, had grins slapped across their faces. You'd think this was for *him*.

He glanced at Anna, hoping she would help him know what to do, what to say. As if reading his mind and realizing he was completely out of his league at an event like this, she crossed the room. "I guess you never expected to have a baby shower."

"No, I have to admit, something like that never even crossed my mind."

"As much as we hate seeing you and Jessica move home," Joy said, "we realize it's time you did. And since we knew you didn't have the opportunity to purchase everything you'd need, we thought it'd be fun to help you. It also gave us an excuse to throw a party."

Sam made his way toward Joy and slipped his arm around her. "I know Jessie's been sleeping in that little bed in the ranch office, but she's going to need something bigger before you know it. So Joy and I bought a crib, along with sheets and a comforter."

"We kept the receipt," Joy added as she pointed out the baby bed that someone had set up near the fireplace.

Nate shook his head, dazed by their generosity, and said, "That won't be necessary. This one will do just fine."

"I hope you like the bedding," Joy said. "I didn't

want to choose anything that would lock you into a color scheme. But that butterfly print with the daisies is both bright and feminine. And don't worry. We can take care of dismantling it so you can transport it to your house."

"I don't know what to say, other than thank you. This is not only mind-boggling, it's very much appreciated." Nate turned to Anna. "Jessie ought to love the colors. What do you think? "

"I think it's perfect." Anna, who was wearing a pair of jeans and a light green T-shirt, blended nicely with the pastel colors, too. And for a moment…

No, Nate wasn't going to go there. Anna was only going to be a temporary sitter.

"Now that our guest of honor has arrived, let's eat." Joy pointed toward the food spread out on the table buffet style. "Nate, why don't you and Anna fill your plates first?"

Unable to think of an argument, especially since he'd worked up an appetite this afternoon, he placed his hand on Anna's back, and they headed for the stack of paper plates, napkins and plasticware.

A white tablecloth covered the table, which had been adorned with two pink Western bandannas. A Mason jar filled with daisies sat on each of them. But it was the amazing array of food that stood out to Nate.

What a spread. Joy had been busy preparing fried chicken, potato salad, a fruit platter and a variety of side dishes. As Anna started down the line, serving herself, Nate followed suit.

Right behind them, Joy and a nurse's aide began to fill plates for a couple of the retired cowboys who didn't get around very well, followed by the others who were eager to serve themselves in what amounted to a Western feast.

The chairs that filled the room were pretty much taken, so Nate sat on the living room sofa, next to Anna.

"We obviously were able to pull this off and surprise you," she said.

"You got that right. I never expected anything like it. How big of a part did you play in all of this?"

"It was Joy's idea. I just helped a little."

"What'd you do?" he asked. "Decorate?" He doubted she'd helped out in the kitchen because Joy had such a good handle on the meals, including any food prep.

Anna brightened, a dazzling smile lighting her hazel eyes. "Yes, and I also planned the games."

"Seriously?" He set his plate on his knees then reached for a glass of fruit punch. "You mean, we're going to do more than just eat?"

"Yep. Just wait and see. It'll be fun. Then you get to open the presents."

This was unbelievable—and so unexpected. Nate wasn't sure if he should be pleased or embarrassed. Both, he supposed. But he found himself to be especially glad to be seated next to Anna.

After everyone had eaten their fill, the games began. First up was a race to diaper a baby doll while wearing a yellow Western bandanna as a blindfold.

Caroline, one of the nurse's aides who had four children of her own, won hands down.

"I learned to change my little ones in the dark so they wouldn't wake up," she explained. "I'm pretty fast, too."

Apparently, Nate thought. For her speedy efforts, she won a box of chocolates. She was also rewarded with a vanilla-scented candle for neatness.

Anna proceeded to give them the rules for the next game as she passed out paper and pens to anyone wanting to play. "You have three minutes to list every song you can think of that has the word *baby* in the title."

Raul Santiago, who'd once played in a country-western band, took the prize that time, listing twenty-three songs, only two of which were disputed by a couple of the other guests. He won a bag of Jolly Rancher candies.

The last competition of the evening involved ten brown lunch sacks that had been sealed shut. Each one contained something a baby needed. The object of the game was to feel the item through the paper and guess what was inside.

This time around, Gilbert Henry, whose late wife once operated a day care in their home, was able to guess all but one of them.

When Anna announced that Gil's prize was a 100 Grand candy bar, one of the oldsters requested a loan, which led to a lot of chuckles.

Then they gave everything in the bags—which included things like a pacifier, a bottle, a jar of baby food and a tiny nail clipper—to Nate. Since he never would have thought to purchase those things, it only served to further convince him that he wasn't the least bit ready to parent Jessie on his own.

After the cake was cut—vanilla with chocolate filling and buttercream frosting—Anna offered to help Joy clean up.

"That's not necessary," the cook said. "There's not much to do in the kitchen. I was able to put the left-overs away while the games were going on."

"In that case, I'd better hit the road." Anna reached for her purse. "I'd really like to get home before it gets much later."

Home. To Nate's house.

He shook off the warmth those words had triggered. "I'll walk you to the car." Then he followed her out the door and onto the porch.

"I can't imagine needing anything else for her," he said.

Anna laughed. "You certainly have enough to tide you over for the time being."

"Then I'll load up this stuff after I finish work tomorrow and bring the baby home with me." The whole idea of being solely responsible still bothered him, but he'd become adept at feeding and changing her.

He'd yet to give her a bath, though.

Anna reached out and placed her hand on his upper arm, sending a jolt of heat to the bone and causing his biceps to flex and tighten. "You look scared."

He hadn't meant to be so transparent, but he recovered and shook it off. His expression, that is, but not Anna's gentle, reassuring touch. "I'm just a little apprehensive about something going wrong, but I'll be fine. Besides, like I told you, I live close to the medical center. And on tcp of that, you'll be at the house until the new nanny starts."

"Yes, I will. So I'd better get started on finding someone qualified to look after Jessie while you work. I'll also have the art studio cleared out before you get home."

As if realizing she was still touching him, she withdrew her hand, her fingers trailing along his sleeve, taking the warmth along with them.

"I'd better go," she said. "I have a lot to do before you get there tomorrow. And don't worry about dinner. I'll figure out something, although I can't promise it'll be able to compete with anything Joy can make."

"I hadn't meant to work you to the bone."

She laughed again, the lilt of her voice perking up his sense of hearing, just as her touch had jolted his arm.

It almost made him eager to pack his canvas bag with his belongings, load Jessie's gifts into the bed of his pickup and head home.

As Anna turned to go, to head back to 331 Peachtree Lane, Nate had a feeling his house would never be the same again. He just hoped the change would be a good one.

Chapter Eight

Late the next afternoon, after loading the baby gifts in the bed of his pickup and placing Jessie in her car seat, where it was secured in the back of his king cab, Nate headed to his house on Peachtree Lane.

Since Jessie's tummy was full and her diaper was dry, she dozed off before he'd even turned onto the county road. If his luck held out, she'd sleep all the way home.

Home. He liked the sound of that, the image it provoked. Peace, refuge. Smiles and laughter.

Family.

Could he make it work? Could he create the kind of loving environment Jessie deserved when, as a child, Nate had never really had anything like that?

Sure, he could. He had Anna to help him get

started, and before long, he'd have a competent nanny to run the household while he was at the Rocking C.

And speaking of the ranch, Nate hadn't planned to work there forever. When he first accepted the job offer, he'd told Sam it was temporary, that he'd stick around until he figured out what he wanted to do with the rest of his life. But now he was committed to running things while Sam was on his honeymoon—and it didn't sound like Sam was in any hurry to get back. If he thought he was going to retire and that Nate would take over, he had another think coming. Because the minute Sam returned, Nate was going to move on. He needed to find a job closer to home.

He had a daughter to think about now, and he didn't like the idea of being so far away from her for such a long period of time. Considering the commute, he'd be gone for ten to twelve hours a day if he stayed at the Rocking C. So that was no longer an option.

What if Jessie needed him? Not that Nate had any idea what to do if there was any kind of pediatric emergency. That's what the nanny was for. But Nate was the one with legal custody, the one who'd be making the decisions, the one who'd…

The one who'd be worried sick if something ever happened to her.

God, what if it did?

Whenever he thought about the many things that could go wrong, like an illness or accident or anything else, his gut twisted and his heart damn near jumped out of his chest. Who knew when a calamity—minor or otherwise—might strike?

Nate had certainly experienced plenty of unexpected blows when he'd been younger. Hell, life-changing events still came his way.

Thankfully, Nate had learned to roll with the punches, but Jessie was too small, too vulnerable. She needed him to protect her, and he couldn't very well do that from a distance.

Warring thoughts and concerns bombarded him all the way to town. As he turned into his neighborhood and neared his house, he saw that Anna had parked her car along the curb in front, leaving the driveway for him. He appreciated her thoughtfulness, as well as her willingness to help.

After shutting off the ignition, he unsnapped the baby carrier from the base and took a sleeping Jessie inside, planning to unload the gifts later.

The moment he opened the front door, the rich and hearty aroma of tomatoes, basil and Italian spices assaulted him. Talk about surprises. If that hunger-stirring, mouthwatering smell meant anything at all, Anna's culinary skill might match Joy's.

Anna, who must have heard the door squeak open, entered the living room wearing a smile. She'd pulled her long, blond hair into a messy topknot and was dressed casually in a white T-shirt and black yoga pants. Her feet, with that cotton-candy pink toenail polish, were bare.

A man could get used to coming home like this, to being met by a woman like her. But Nate tossed aside that notion as quickly as it came to mind. Anna was only here because she needed temporary lodging and Nate needed her to help him create a safe place to raise a baby.

"Aw," she said, crossing the living room and making her way toward him. "Jessie's home."

Actually, so was Nate. But he ignored the wounded little kid inside him, the one that sometimes rose up and clamored to be included. Instead, he smiled and said, "Whatever's on the stove sure smells good. You weren't kidding when you said you'd 'do something' about dinner."

"I've been busy all day. And not just in the kitchen." She tossed him a hundred-watt grin. "Wait until I show you what I've done to the nursery. Come on. Follow me upstairs."

Nate set the carrier with the sleeping baby on the floor near the sofa then proceeded up to the second floor behind Anna. As he watched the gentle sway of her hips, the thoughts he'd been having about coming home took on a different slant, a romantic one. But a relationship with Anna, no matter how short-lived their time together might be, was sure to plummet before it got too far off the ground.

When they reached the doorway to what had once been Audrey's art studio, Nate looked inside. The room was now empty, other than the small dresser that used to be near the closet and had been moved next to the window. Anna had been busy, all right. She'd also gotten a lot more accomplished than he'd realized.

"At first," she said, "I was going to suggest that you paint the walls to give it a fresh new look. But after I packed everything and moved it out to the shed, I realized you wouldn't need to do anything to this room at all."

She was right. Grandpa Clint and Audrey had only been living in the house for about six months before the accident, and they'd painted before they'd moved in. They'd also put in new flooring.

"Now that the art supplies and easels are gone," Anna said, "the soft green color is a lot more noticeable. It's going to blend nicely with the baby bedding Sam and Joy gave you."

She was right. "I guess I'd better put that crib together so we can set things up in here."

"I can't believe how nicely this is coming together."

"Yes, but I didn't want you to have to work so hard or to lug all that stuff out of the house on your own. I was going to do it tonight, after I got home."

"I know, but it really wasn't much of a chore. I started by purchasing cardboard boxes, then I packed each one lightly, labeled them and carried them out to the shed. I was finished by noon."

"Well, thanks. I really appreciate what you did. Now the only big job will be putting up the crib, which I can do before we eat."

"Why don't you wait until after dinner?" she suggested. "I have a feeling you're probably hungry. I made spaghetti, and it's almost done. All I have to do is boil the pasta."

"Then I'll take a shower and meet you in the kitchen. It won't take me long."

"Perfect!"

What was? The timing? Or Anna?

A loose strand had slipped from her messy top-knot. She also had a small black smudge of mascara under her right eye. But he couldn't spot a single flaw in her. Not with that smile lighting up the amber flecks in her honey-colored eyes. She was not only beautiful, but downright perfect, too, if you asked him.

In fact, he was tempted to ignore any reservations he had about pursuing a romantic relationship with her. But what would he do if things didn't work out?

Or worse, what if they did?

As Anna turned down the hall on her way to the kitchen, and Nate headed to the bathroom, he scratched the idea completely.

Everyone he'd ever cared about had abandoned him in one way or another. What made Nate Gallagher think a woman like Anna Reynolds would consider him to be a keeper?

Anna had never considered herself a cook by any stretch of the imagination. Yet by the way Nate had wolfed down his spaghetti and raved about the taste of her homemade sauce, you'd think she'd been whipping up family meals for years.

She hadn't, of course. She'd actually grown up on convenience foods. But once she'd gone to college, she'd begun eating healthier meals.

One of the girls who'd shared an apartment with her when she'd been in grad school had been a foodie and was always trying new recipes, so Anna had learned a lot from her.

This particular marinara sauce, which was made from olive oil, fresh tomatoes, basil and garlic, had been a favorite of all the girls, especially Anna. And now, as she watched Nate finish a second helping, she suspected he liked the taste as much as she and her roommates had.

She'd just begun to think about clearing the table when little Jessie, who'd been sleeping in the carrier next to them, woke up. By the sound of her wailing, she was clearly hungry and ready to eat.

"I'll change her diaper and give her a bottle," Nate said. "That is, unless you want to do it. If so, I'll clean up the kitchen."

Since Anna had yet to see him interact much with the baby, she said, "No, you go ahead and feed her. I'd rather do the dishes."

He nodded in agreement then carried the baby into the other room, where he'd left her diaper bag.

Since Anna had always been organized and cleaned up after herself as she cooked, the kitchen was in good shape. So it only took her a few minutes to wash the dishes. Once things were tidy, she returned to the living room, where Nate was sitting in a brown leather recliner, holding Jessie as she nursed hungrily on a bottle he'd prepared with water and powdered formula.

She stood in the doorway a moment, watching the rugged cowboy study his daughter while she ate. His brow was furrowed as he held the precious pink bundle close to his chest. It was a sweet sight, one that stirred something deep in Anna's heart. She wasn't quite sure what to call that dormant feeling. A longing, she supposed, for something she'd always needed but never had.

When Nate glanced up and caught her staring at him, a sheepish grin dimpled his cheek. "Do you want to take over for me? That way, I can set up her crib in the nursery."

"Sure." Anna would actually love to hold the baby, to watch her doze off in her arms. "But we'll need to launder the sheet and blanket before we put her to bed."

"Joy washed all the clothes and linens before she packed everything up for me to take home, so we're good to go."

Nate got to his feet while continuing to hold the baby close, the bottle propped up. After he passed Jessie to Anna, they traded places so she could take over the feeding and he could move the crib and everything else from the back of his truck to the nursery.

As he stepped outside, Anna focused her attention on the baby. Yet each time Nate came back into the room, first with the disassembled crib and next with a toolbox, she found her interest split between the handsome man and the precious infant.

Jessie had just about finished eating when Nate carried the mattress into the house. Next he brought in the comforter and a matching butterfly mobile.

"Do you need any help?" Anna asked him, as she

got to her feet, holding Jessie close, and followed him upstairs.

"No, the crib was easy to assemble. But you might want to make sure I put the bedding on right."

Anna watched Nate stretch the white cotton sheet over the mattress. Then he placed the colorful comforter with the butterfly and daisy print on top. She'd been right. The colors really pulled the decor together.

"If you'll draw back the covers, I'll put her in bed."

Nate nodded, then complied.

As Anna lay the sleeping baby in the crib, a spring of warmth bubbled up in her heart and a rush of maternal thoughts churned in her head, feelings that were unusual for a career woman who'd never been especially close to her own mother.

Maybe those feelings were actually just sympathy for Jessie, who didn't have a mother at all. But then again, the little girl *did* have a daddy.

Anna stole a glance at Nate, who was standing beside the crib, looking at his sleeping daughter. Whatever emotion she'd been feeling moments ago, whether it was sympathy or something else, grew stronger, but she fought it off the best she could. There was no way she could get personally involved with this little family. Her stay at Nate's house would be over soon. Besides, she wasn't the domestic or maternal type.

"That's amazing," Nate said.

For a moment she wondered if he'd been reading her mind, but he couldn't possibly know the thoughts and feelings she'd been having.

"What's amazing?" Anna asked.

"The way Jessie's presence in this room has completely chased away Audrey's."

"What do you mean?"

He gave a slight shrug. "I didn't dislike Audrey. It's just that..." He paused as if carefully choosing his words. "When I first moved to the Double M, my grandfather was single. Then, about six months later, he got married. At the time I was actually looking forward to..." Again his words came to a halt for a moment. "Some kids might have resented having someone new move in the house and into their lives, but my mother died when I was pretty young, so I'd thought it might be...cool."

"And it wasn't?"

"It was all right, I guess. But Audrey kept her distance from me. And she had places that were off-limits, like what she called the 'formal' living room, the kitchen and especially the den, which she turned into an art studio. In fact, I couldn't even peek inside that room because the door was always closed."

"Was she mean to you?"

"No. Sometimes I thought she might resent me, but she was just quiet. She also always seemed to be working on one project or another. Either way, she was too busy to be bothered with a kid like me."

"Were you a troublemaker?" Anna asked, wondering what reason the woman could have for avoiding a boy who was practically an orphan.

"I never tried to be. All I'd wanted to do was..." Again Nate's voice drifted to silence. But this time he didn't continue the subject he'd broached. Instead, he said, "I'd better unload the rest of that stuff from my truck." Then, as if he'd never shared his pain, as if he'd never opened up at all, he turned and left the room.

Anna's heart ached for the boy he used to be, as well as the man he'd become, and the memories that still dogged him. As a professional and a social worker, she wanted to know more about his past so she could help him have a better, happier future. And as a woman, she wanted the same thing for another reason, one she didn't dare ponder.

So she scanned the baby's room instead. Just as she'd thought, the pastel colors and the butterfly print of the comforter transformed an unused art studio into a cheerful nursery.

That's amazing, Nate had said. *The way Jessie's presence in this room has suddenly chased away Audrey's.*

Chased away? Nate's choice of words had been interesting, although Anna didn't want to read too much into it.

Audrey was nice enough to me, but we really weren't that close. I doubt there's anything in there that I'd want to keep.

The woman might not have been cruel to him, but withholding love and affection could be just as damaging to a kid as harsh words and a beating.

Anna glanced at little Jessie, hoping she would have everything a girl could ever wish for, including the things that had escaped Anna when she'd been a child.

If Anna were to remain a part of Jessie's life, she'd do everything in her power to make sure her emotional needs were met. But Anna would be moving on soon.

Her gaze drifted to the comforter, to the butterfly print, which seemed to be a perfect choice for a room that had morphed from a cold, forbidden art studio to a loving nursery.

Footsteps sounded on the stairway. Anna turned to see Nate reenter the room carrying two cardboard boxes stacked on top of each other. She assumed they held the assortment of other gifts he'd received at the shower.

"We don't need to put all of this away yet," he said, "especially since Jessie's asleep. But I'd like to set up the baby monitor."

"Good idea."

As Nate dug through one box, Anna spotted a night-light in the other—an angel that would provide a soft light while the baby slept at night. So she removed it and placed it in one of the outlets.

Once Nate had the monitor in place, they stood back and surveyed the nursery.

"Can you believe how quickly this all came together?" he asked, his expression warm and appreciative. "This is the perfect place for the baby to sleep. We make a good team."

"I couldn't agree more." Working together, they'd done a good job. She cast a smile his way, only to watch the warmth in his gaze shift to heated and intense.

She wasn't exactly sure what he was thinking, but she could certainly sense it. And feel it.

While she ought to be unsettled by it—and opposed to it—her heart soared and her breathing slowed to a near standstill.

But she and Nate weren't a team. They'd just worked well together today. His real teammate would be the nanny he was about to hire. Yet every nerve ending in her body rose up in a cheer, as if she'd just been chosen as his first-round draft pick.

A rebellious surge of pride filled her, insisting she was the only teammate he'd ever need.

He lifted his hand and cupped her jaw. His thumb brushed against her cheek, sending a spiral of heat rippling through her and stealing every bit of common sense she'd ever possessed.

"Thanks for all your help," he said. "I'm not sure what I would have done without you."

It had been the polite thing for him to say, but his eyes, his hand and that blasted caress of his thumb were sending another message completely.

She managed to mutter, "You're welcome," even though her best response would be to step back and regroup. But with the intensity of his gaze turning her inside out, the best she could do was to close her eyes and hope that by doing so she could somehow break whatever invisible thread had woven between them.

Her efforts weren't working, though. Even after she'd blinked a few times, he continued to hold her captive, strengthening whatever bond stretched between them.

All at once his thumb stilled, and his hand slid from her face. Surprisingly, even though he no longer touched her, the lingering heat his hand left behind threatened to burn bright all night long.

"I have an early day tomorrow," he said. "I'd better turn in."

Fearing any words she might try to say would just wad up in her throat, she nodded and took a step back.

"Do you need anything before I go?" he asked.

Until he'd touched her, she'd forgotten any "needs" she'd ever had. And now that he'd stirred up the feminine longings she'd been neglecting for what seemed like forever…

No, she didn't dare let a crazy, misguided thought like that take root in her heart or her mind.

"I'm fine," she said. "I'm going to take a shower and go to bed. I have a book I'd like to read, and this is a good night to start it." On the other hand, starting something with the handsome cowboy daddy wasn't a viable option.

"Then good night," he said, tossing her a crooked grin. "Sleep tight."

She managed to return his smile before slipping out of the nursery and into the hall. If she knew what was good for her, she'd move back to the Night Owl Motel right now—or at least, first thing in the morning.

But she'd made an agreement to help Nate find a

qualified nanny, and she would stick to her part of the deal.

Even if it threatened to be her undoing.

What in the hell were you thinking, Gallagher? Touching Anna like that was a big mistake. A huge *one.*

Nate remained in the nursery long after Anna entered the guest room and closed the door. Things were moving way too fast, and not just with the baby, who'd dozed off as though she belonged here.

She did, of course. Belong *here*. This house would be her home, even if Nate could hardly imagine things coming together like that.

But it wouldn't be Anna's home. And as sure as Nate was about that, he'd almost done something stupid during the heat of the moment, almost suggested something completely out of the question.

Not that he intended to be celibate for the rest of his life. He'd date again someday, when the time was right, when Jessie was older and he'd gotten a good, solid grip on family life. But right now his focus had to be on the baby girl he'd accepted as his own.

Nate might not live up to be the kind of daddy she needed or deserved, but he'd be a lot better father than the one he'd had.

And that thing with Anna, the feelings and urges she'd stirred up inside him? That was just a result of raging hormones and lust caused by a fleeting rush of testosterone after he'd shared an awesome spaghetti dinner with a beautiful blonde, a woman who'd gone above and beyond to help him create a cozy nursery for his daughter to come home to.

For a couple of heartbeats, he'd almost let his appreciation and his imagination get the better of him. But he had that under control now. All he had to do was shake off the lingering urge to kiss Anna senseless, to see where desire might lead them.

Another shower might help—a cold one this time. But first he double-checked the baby monitor and carried the receiver into his bedroom.

He couldn't possibly consider a romantic relationship right now, especially with Anna.

Only trouble was, long after he'd turned in for the night, he continued to think about the pretty social worker sleeping down the hall. As a result, he didn't doze off until nearly midnight.

He'd set the alarm on his cell phone to wake him at four o'clock the next morning, but he hadn't needed to. Jessie's cry practically shook the rafters when she woke up just before three, hungry and screaming for a bottle.

Nate hurried to the nursery, only to find Anna had beat him there. She was picking up the unhappy baby and shushing her. "Don't cry, sweetie. I have you."

Nate ought to step inside and offer to help. Instead, he leaned against the doorjamb and watched the woman and child. Anna might not have any kids of her own, but she seemed to know instinctively what to do.

So now what?

At one time he'd been afraid to take Jessie home, but that wasn't what scared him now.

How in the hell was he going to survive living in the same house with Anna until he hired a permanent nanny, especially when he needed to keep his hands to himself?

Chapter Nine

Over the next few days Nate and Anna settled into a comfortable and easy routine. He continued to work at the ranch and was away from home more often than not, but he began to look forward to each evening, when he could expect to have a hearty meal and a happy baby.

While Anna cleaned the kitchen, he fed and bathed Jessie before putting her to bed. Then, after the dishes were done and the baby fell asleep, Nate and Anna would turn on the television and watch old movies. It was actually nice to come home now, and in spite of his resolve to keep his distance from his temporary roommate and sitter, he had to admit that Anna had become rather special to him.

She also did what she'd promised to do. She'd lined

up several potential nannies to interview, and on Saturday morning the first one arrived at the house.

When Nate answered the door, he found a matronly woman in her midfifties on the stoop. "You must be Barbara Newcomb."

"Yes, I am."

He stepped aside. "Please come in."

Barbara, who wore a turquoise blouse, black slacks and sensible shoes, entered the living room with a warm smile.

"This is Anna Reynolds," Nate said, introducing the two women. "She's my…" Anna had certainly become more than a roommate or a sitter, although he wasn't sure how much more. But he couldn't very well let his sentence dangle, so he offered the only other option readily available. "She's a social worker and also…my friend."

"It's nice to meet you," Barbara said before returning her attention to Nate. "I may not have a list of former employers to give you, but I do have references, like the pastor of my church and the principals of all the schools my children once attended. This job would actually be my first as a nanny, but don't worry. I have plenty of experience running a household and caring for babies."

Nate had yet to review any of the applications, although he planned to carefully go over each one this weekend.

"Barbara's daughter is away at college," Anna told Nate. "Her son is in the army and stationed in Germany."

The older woman's smile broadened. "Jeremy and his wife have two little ones, a toddler and a kindergartener. Since they're stationed out of the country, I don't get to see them as often as I'd like to, so I'm looking forward to taking care of other children. I'll love and cuddle them until I can be with my own grandkids."

Nate actually liked the idea that she wasn't in her twenties and that her experience was that of a real mother, one who'd raised a son who'd joined the military and a daughter in college. It also sounded as if she had a couple of good references. He'd call each of them, of course. But so far, he liked Barbara Newcomb.

He and Anna chatted with her for several minutes. They learned that she'd been a widow for nearly three years, but that she'd been happily married to a man she referred to as the love of her life.

Before Nate could thank her for coming and tell her he'd be in touch, Jessie's cry sounded upstairs.

"Oh," Barbara said. "The baby's awake. I'd love to meet her—if that's okay."

That actually sounded like a good idea. Nate would like to see how the woman related to Jessie. "I'll bring her downstairs."

"And I'll fix a bottle," Anna said. "She's a lot happier—and more social—when her tummy is full."

Minutes later Nate had changed Jessie's diaper, brought her down to the living room and placed her in Barbara's open arms. As soon as Anna handed over the bottle, Barbara offered it to the crying baby, who quickly latched on to the nipple.

"She's absolutely precious," Barbara said.

Nate had to agree. Jessie was still a tiny thing, but she was growing and filling out. With tufts of dark hair and blue eyes, she promised to be a real cutie when she finally began to toddle around.

As the grandmotherly woman continued to coo and make a fuss over Jessie, Nate's confidence level grew. He wasn't yet convinced that he'd found the right nanny, but he was beginning to think that Barbara Newcomb just might fit the bill.

He glanced at Anna. As if sensing his gaze and his unasked question, she looked his way and smiled. Apparently, she was thinking along the same lines he was.

When Jessie had finished her bottle, Nate thanked Barbara for coming. "We still have a couple of other interviews scheduled," he said, "but I'll be in touch."

Barbara smiled then took one last look at Jessie before handing her over to Nate. "I'll look forward to hearing from you."

After Anna escorted the first nanny candidate to the door, she turned to Nate and smiled. "So what do you think?"

He was about to say he liked Barbara a lot, so much that he might not even need to interview anyone else, but he held back. Anna was a trained social worker. Maybe she'd picked up on something he'd missed.

"You go first," he said.

"All right. I like her. We'll have to talk to her references, of course. But the agency has already vetted her, and she's bonded. So I think you should seriously consider her for the job."

A smile of relief stretched across his face. "Good. That's exactly what I was thinking."

As much as Nate wanted to celebrate the fact that his nanny search might be over almost as soon as it began, he couldn't find it in himself to rejoice. For one thing, once the new nanny moved in and got settled, Anna would be leaving.

And for some crazy reason, in spite of the uneasiness and apprehension he'd felt when he'd first met her, he wasn't ready to see her go.

On Monday afternoon, before Nate returned from the ranch, Anna's cell phone rang. It was her landlord.

"Hello," Carla said. "I'm glad I found you. I tried your number at work first, and they said you were on vacation."

"I didn't leave town," Anna said. "I'm staying with a friend. How are things coming along at the apartment?"

"Actually, it's going much better now. The workers are finally making some real progress, and you should be able to move back in by Friday morning—maybe even sooner. You've been such a good tenant that I wanted to let you know before you found another place to live."

"Thanks for the update," Anna said. "That's good news. My friend said I can stay as long as I need to, but I don't want to take advantage of his kindness much longer."

That was true, of course. But Friday might be a little too soon to move out since she'd promised Nate she would stay until after he hired a nanny and the woman got settled.

Anna loved her studio apartment and wanted to return, but admittedly, she wasn't as eager to go home as she'd once been. She'd fallen into a comfortable situation while staying with Nate. She also enjoyed having a baby to care for, to talk to. And that was saying something for a woman who'd never liked to play with dolls when she'd been a little girl.

Who would have thought that Anna had a domestic side? She certainly hadn't realized it, and while being with Nate and Jessie was a nice change of pace, it wouldn't last. She loved her job at the hospital and had no intention of giving it up.

"I'll call you as soon as you can move in," Carla said.

Anna thanked her then said goodbye. After placing her cell back into her purse, she returned to the kitchen to check on the roast beef in the oven.

Tonight's dessert, homemade apple crisp, was cooling on the counter. There was vanilla ice cream in the freezer, which she planned to put on top of each serving.

She'd no more than refried the homemade pinto beans she'd made earlier when the front door creaked open and shut.

"I'm home," Nate called out.

A thrill of excitement shot through her. She tried to tamp it down, but wasn't having much luck. She was glad Nate was back and looking forward to hearing what he had to say about tonight's menu.

After turning off the flame under the skillet, she placed the wooden spoon in the sink and went to the living room to greet him as if falling into a domestic role wasn't the least bit out of the ordinary.

Yet she couldn't deny the rush of satisfaction she took in having Nate home, in knowing he would appreciate her efforts at creating a hungry man's meal.

"Hey!" she said as if his arrival had surprised her. "Did you have a good day?"

"It was okay. How's Jessie?"

"Sound asleep. I took her outside for a walk this afternoon. She really seemed to enjoy looking around and checking out her neighborhood. You should have seen her."

"I wish I had."

Seriously? That was just what she'd been hoping for—to know he'd bonded with his daughter. To know that Jessie had a loving daddy and a happy home.

Sure, some kids didn't. But *this* little girl…?

As much as Anna hoped to keep her distance and not get too involved with a patient or her family, she'd been drawn to Jessie since day one.

She'd also been drawn to her daddy.

Nate removed his worn Stetson and hung it on a hook near the door. His hair was mussed, and his blue eyes sparked with something bright, something she couldn't quite name but looked forward to seeing each night.

As he sauntered across the hardwood floor, all lean and male and cowboy, Anna's heart spun out in her chest. She hated to admit it, but she'd been waiting for this moment all day long.

Wait. That wasn't quite true. She was making it into something more than it really was. She'd just spent the past twelve hours with an infant who couldn't talk to her. She'd only been looking for some adult conversation. That's all it was.

"Where is she?" he asked.

The baby? Yes, of course. It was all about Jessie—as it *should* be.

"She's upstairs in her crib. We had a great afternoon. She's staying awake for longer periods of time now."

"I assume that's good," Nate said.

"Yes, of course."

He spotted the novel she'd left on the lamp table, near the easy chair. "*Moby Dick*?"

Anna shrugged. "I hope you don't mind, but I found it in the bookcase."

"You like to read?"

"Yes, I love books." In fact, after taking a creative writing course in college, she'd thought about writing the great American novel. But she hadn't considered it very long. She knew it wouldn't be easy to complete a manuscript—or to find an agent or publisher. And after realizing she'd had enough uncertainty and instability in her life, she'd changed her major from English Lit to psychology.

Nate nodded at the book. "It's a great story. You're going to like it."

"I didn't realize we had the love of reading in common." She pointed to the built-in bookcase. "That's an impressive selection of novels."

"They were Audrey's."

Anna's expression must have fallen because he quickly added, "Not that I haven't read some of them. I had a lot of downtime while my bones were mending. But now, by the time I get home, I'm usually too tired to do much of anything except eat and shower."

At that, she smiled. "Then maybe I'd better get dinner on the table."

"Sounds good to me." He tossed her a grin that set off a flutter in her belly. "What're we having tonight?"

"Shredded beef tacos." She tucked a loose strand of hair behind her ear. "I hope that's okay."

"You bet. I love Mexican food."

They studied each other for a moment, and as a weird sense of awkwardness settled over them, Anna was reminded of those silly junior high dances where the girls lined one wall of the cafeteria while the boys huddled together on the other.

Yet it wasn't just nervous energy sparking in the room. There also seemed to be a flurry of hormones and pheromones swirling around them.

Anna wished that the baby would cry, signaling the need for a diaper change, a bottle or some cuddling—

anything to take the adults' attention from whatever was going on between them right now. But Jessie, who'd been up for nearly two hours before falling asleep just minutes before, wasn't cooperating.

"I have to—" Anna nodded toward the kitchen "—check the meat and fry the corn tortillas. Everything else is ready."

"Then I'll take a shower," Nate said. "That is, unless you have something else you want me to do."

The only thing she could think of him doing was to cup her jaw again, to brush his thumb across her cheek, to look deep in her eyes and to…

Get a grip, she told herself before telling Nate, "I don't need any help. I have everything under control."

That is, everything but her thoughts, emotions and hormones. She could almost imagine herself spending her days rocking a baby or pushing a stroller then fixing dinner each night for a handsome cowboy.

The vision was far too domestic for her own good, especially when she'd never had a solid family of her own—or even a good maternal role model.

Anna's mom had never been one to care about recipes or keeping the house tidy. In fact, about ten years ago, after her parents divorced, her mother had remarried a drummer in a rock band. The two had had a daughter together and seemed happy, but they lived in a messy house on a busy street. And even though Anna tried to go "home" for a visit once or twice a year, there was nothing homey about it.

On the other hand, Nate's house…

Darn it. Maternal longings and romantic thoughts

were going to sweep her away if she wasn't careful. So she'd have to do something about it—and quick.

Instead of watching television with Nate, which had become a habit and a lot more appealing than it should be, she would go to her room and read. Captain Ahab's story would be far better than the tales she kept spinning on her own, especially one that included a handsome cowboy hero.

Thank goodness the studio apartment would be ready for her soon. She had to get out of here before her own obsession left her with a worse fate than that of a crazed sea captain determined to capture a white whale that would be the death of him.

Anna had set up two more interviews, one on Tuesday evening and the second on Wednesday. While Nate liked both women, he'd pretty much made up his mind to hire Barbara Newcomb, especially after talking to her references.

Apparently, she sang in the church choir, taught vacation Bible school each summer and headed up the yearly church mission trip to an orphanage in Mexico. In addition to that, she'd spent several different terms as the president of the PTA and had also been a classroom volunteer at the elementary and middle school levels. So as far as Nate was concerned, the decision had been made.

Barbara Newcomb would be moving into his home, and Anna would be leaving.

So why wasn't he feeling the least bit relieved?

Because something had happened between them the

other night. And he had no idea what—if anything—to do about it.

After Anna had first moved in, they'd become friends, the kind that laughed and teased each other. He'd looked forward to going home to her each night, and before he knew it, he'd gotten caught up in something totally unexpected.

Now things were different between them. Their smiles and gazes were heated instead of warm, their conversations strained rather than comfortable.

Sure, the meals Anna made were just as good. In fact, if he didn't know better, he'd think that she'd whipped them up with him in mind. In any case, he called her at noon today and told her not to cook, that he'd be bringing dinner to her.

So after placing an order ahead of time, he'd stopped by Maestro's on Main Street and picked up a sausage pizza, a vegetarian antipasto salad for two, breadsticks and cannoli. Then he took it home.

When he entered the house, he found her curled up on the sofa, a book in her hand.

"Hi," she said, setting the novel on the lamp table. "Let me help you with that."

"I've got it." He bumped the door shut with his shoulder then carried the pizza box and bags inside.

She got to her feet anyway. Then she crossed the room and reached out to take some of his load. "What'd you bring?"

"Pizza, salad, dessert."

"That sounds great. Do you want to eat first, while it's still warm?"

That might be best, but he needed a shower. Things might be awkward between them these days, but he wanted to be at his best when he was with her.

"I won't be long," he said. "Just give me a couple of minutes."

And that was about all it took for him to take a hot shower and change into clean clothes.

Anna had no more than set the food on the table when he entered the kitchen. "I've got a bottle of red wine in the pantry," he said. "I feel like celebrating. Why don't we open it and have a glass?"

"All right. But what's the big occasion?"

"I've decided to hire Barbara."

"That's great. I think she'll be perfect for you."

He hoped she was right, that Barbara would be as good for him and Jessie as Anna had been the past few days. Only trouble was, that meant Anna would be leaving soon.

"Any word about your house?" he asked.

"Actually, yes. My landlord said it might be ready for me to move back in on Friday."

So soon? He tried to keep his expression neutral, although he didn't know how successful he'd been.

"But don't worry," Anna said. "I won't leave until after Barbara can move in and get settled."

Thank goodness for that. "I'd appreciate it if you would."

"Of course. I've gotten pretty fond of Jessie, especially after being with her all day. She's a beautiful baby."

"I think so, but I'm probably biased."

"You have every right to be. After all, she's your daughter."

Yes, but he and Jessie weren't necessarily blood kin. Did that make a difference? He hoped it wouldn't. Maybe DNA didn't have anything to do with it. After all, Nate and his own father might have had a remarkable physical resemblance to each other, but they were nothing alike. And they'd had a lousy relationship.

"Hey," Anna said, "I was just thinking."

Whatever she had on her mind had put a spark in her eyes, making the amber flecks shine like gold.

"About what?"

"About staying in touch with you after I move on. If Barbara ever needs to take some time off, I could… you know, step in and watch Jessie for you."

"I'd like that."

Her smile deepened, and as she gazed at him, drawing him into the depths of her eyes, he realized a man could…

What? Fall for a woman like her?

He could certainly see that happening to any man, even to him. But on the other hand, that didn't mean a college-educated professional like Anna would find a broken-down ranch hand appealing. Besides, something told him she'd be looking for a lifetime match, which was too bad since Nate didn't believe in forever and always.

He did, however, believe in making the most of the present, and if any woman had ever tempted him to strike up a little romance for an evening, it was the beautiful blonde standing before him.

"What are you thinking about?" she asked. "You seem to be pondering something long and hard."

Oh, he was thinking all right. And without considering the consequences, he closed the short distance between them.

Her eyes widened and her lips parted in surprise, but she didn't step back or make any move to stop him, which was all the invitation he needed.

Chapter Ten

The last thing in the world Anna had expected Nate to do tonight was to kiss her. That is, until he eased toward her, his blue eyes lit up with heat and locked on her.

She could have objected. In fact, she probably should have, but for some inexplicable reason she slipped her arms around his neck and lifted her mouth to his. She might be sorry about this later. She'd probably have a slew of regrets when it was all over, but none of that mattered because she couldn't have moved away if she'd wanted to. Instead, she lost herself in the heady scent of his musky cologne.

His lips pressed against hers with an urgency that nearly stole her breath away. When his tongue swept into her mouth, she relished the taste of peppermint and hungered for more.

As his hands caressed her back and traveled down the slope of her derriere, she all but melted. And when he pulled her flush against his erection, her mind spun out of control, tangling her thoughts and emotions into one hot mess.

Had she ever been kissed like this?

No, never. Certainly not to the point that she'd become both weak-kneed and addle-brained.

For the first time in her life, Anna wanted to throw caution to the wind, to forget about dreams and plans, to disregard questions of right or wrong. Her only viable option was to let things run their course with a handsome cowboy at the helm.

And what a course they took. As the kiss intensified, desire flared. The power and strength of it might have knocked her to the floor if she hadn't held Nate tightly, determined to remain in his arms or to take him down with her.

What made this kiss, with this man, so good, so special? Surely it was only a physical reaction easily explained by a combination of human chemistry and biology. But that wasn't all she was feeling for Nate.

About the time she thought she'd die from sexual need and the emptiness that ached in her core, Nate tore his lips from hers. Thankfully, he didn't release her or step back. Instead, he rested his forehead against hers, his breathing as ragged as her own.

"I'm not sure what to do about this," he said.

For one thing, he could leave the room and take

his peppermint taste and his musky scent with him. But that wasn't likely. And if truth be told, she didn't want him to go anywhere.

They probably should take things slowly, though. That kiss had left her dizzy and scrambling to figure out what she wanted to do about it.

"I can make us some tea or coffee," she said, hoping that having a chore to do would provide her with time to think. "I also found another bottle of wine in your pantry."

"You want to have something to drink? *Now?*"

No, not really. She'd just thrown out a suggestion, as lame as it was. "I thought we should…you know, talk it over."

"You might be right, but I think sex is best played out—and not debated."

Good point. She combed her fingers through her hair then decided to be completely honest with him. "I want to make love with you—more than I'd realized. I'm just…"

"Concerned about where it might lead?"

Wasn't he?

"Yes," she admitted. "That's what I meant."

"It's up to you, Anna. If you want to see where that kiss might lead, I'm game. And if you'd rather not be lovers, then that's okay, too."

"Is it *really* okay?" she asked, doubting his response. "After we kissed like that, you wouldn't care if I just wanted to remain friends?"

"I wouldn't have a choice. I'd have to deal with your decision. But the way I see it, at this point, it's going to be almost impossible to go back to just being friends."

He was right, but that didn't make their dilemma any easier to face.

"Can I give this some thought?" she asked.

"Of course. I'll be in my room—if you decide you'd like to join me."

Actually, she'd like to take their kisses to the bedroom, but making the progression from friends to lovers wasn't something to be taken lightly.

So she thanked him for the chance to think it over, left him in the kitchen then climbed the stairs and slipped into her own bedroom to freshen up. For what reason, she wasn't entirely sure, but after brushing her teeth and combing her hair, she returned to the hallway, only to hear country music playing from his room—something soft and slow.

Did she dare continue? Was making love with Nate what she actually wanted?

Just reaching this point makes it impossible to go back...

She could still turn around and return to her room, but why? She knew what she wanted, what she craved. What was there to think over, other than the changes sex might have on their lives?

I think sex is best played out—and not debated...

She could toss a coin if she had one handy, but that wasn't necessary. She knew what she wanted, what she needed to do. So she moved to his open doorway, saw him stretched out on top of the forest green comforter, his boots off, his feet bare.

As if sensing her presence, he turned. The hint of a smile crossed his face, and he rolled out of bed and made his way toward her. "I'm glad you're here."

"I'm not sure if this is a good idea."

"Sounds like a great one to me." He cupped her face. "Just so there aren't any misunderstandings, I want to be completely up front with you. I can't give you all the things you need and deserve, but I can give you right now."

She could have asked him to be more specific, but she assumed he was talking about financial security, especially on a ranch hand's pay. But the money or lack of it really didn't matter. She had a solid job.

He might not know it now, but her actual needs revolved around love and family, something he did have, something he *could* give her. She'd seen him with Jessie, watched him feed and change that precious babe as if she were a tiny princess.

Nate was going to be a great father. And Anna had a feeling he'd make a wonderful husband—if that was the direction things went after tonight.

But right now she'd settle for a good lover—and Nate had given her every reason to believe he'd be amazing.

So she stepped into his arms, and he drew her close. This was it. She was determined to go all the way, to hold nothing back. To risk it all—her heart and her soul.

He pressed his lips against her hair. "You smell so good."

"It's the lilac fragrance of my shampoo." She had

a thing for floral scents—that one in particular. What she didn't say was that she'd applied a matching lotion while she'd been in her room, that she'd done it just for him.

She pulled him back to her for another sizzling kiss, one she hoped would never end. As their bodies pressed together, they stroked and caressed each other.

Nate slipped his hand to her breast, kneading the fullness. His thumb skimmed across her nipple, setting off a spiral of heat that surged deep in her most feminine part.

He wasn't just skilled, he was a good lover—the best, she suspected. Coming to his room tonight had been the right decision for her to make. He might not see a future in store for them, but she did. It was burning bright with promise.

All Anna had to do was convince Nate that *he* was all she'd ever need.

As Nate and Anna stood beside his bed, he kissed her again—long and deep. His hands slid along the curve of her back and down the slope of her hips. All the while, his tongue twisted and mated with hers until a surge of desire shot through him like a bullet train.

Fortunately, he kept a stash of condoms handy, although it had been a long time since he'd needed one. He never took chances, although just being with Anna, talking to her and spilling some of his deepest hurts and secrets seemed pretty damned risky.

He'd had plenty of disappointments in life and had made a few mistakes. He just hoped making love with her tonight wouldn't be one of them.

Sex he could handle, especially if it was a one-time thing. But Anna deserved more from a relationship than that. And he had a feeling that what they were about to do wouldn't just happen once. That realization ought to scare the crap out of him, but for some reason, it didn't. He could get used to making love with her over and over again.

He pulled Anna's hips forward, letting her know how much he wanted her, how ready he was to lay her on his bed. She pressed her pelvis against him, taunting his erection. Still, they continued to kiss, to caress and stroke each other until all he wanted to do was to strip off their clothing, which hampered their sexual exploration.

Nate was just about ready to scoop her into his arms and carry her to bed when Anna ended the kiss. Surely she wasn't having second thoughts. He could see why she might change her mind, though.

Neither of them said a word, but she responded to his unasked question by taking his hand and leading him to the edge of the bed. There, she slowly peeled off her feminine T-shirt and dropped it on the floor, revealing a white, lacy bra.

As she reached for the waistband of her pants, unsnapping them, he stood in erotic anticipation, marveling at her curves and watching as she slid the fabric over her hips and down her legs, leaving her in a sexy pair of white panties he'd like to remove himself.

Damn, she was even more beautiful than he'd thought. His imagination hadn't done her body justice. She was a goddess, it seemed. And tonight she was his.

Following her lead, he unbuttoned his shirt, pulled his arms out of the sleeves and let the garment fall to the floor. Next he unbuckled his belt and undid the metal buttons on his jeans.

When he'd removed all but his boxer briefs, she turned and lifted her blond locks so he could unhook her bra. As he freed her breasts, she pushed the white, lacy straps over her shoulders and turned back to face him.

He took full advantage of the lovely sight, of the perfection of her femininity, of the fullness of her breasts. The dusky-pink nipples were taut with arousal, begging to be fondled and kissed. So he dropped to his knees and took one in his mouth. He used his tongue and his hands until she gasped in pleasure, clutching his shoulder to stay balanced.

Taking mercy on her, as well as himself, he lifted her in his arms and placed her on top of the bed. Her hair splayed upon the forest green pillow sham, her body upon the comforter. She reminded him of a fairy princess—or maybe a leprechaun queen able to grant his every wish, his every desire.

"You're beautiful, Anna. I knew you would be."

A slow smile stretched across her lips. "So are you, Nate."

He didn't know about that. His body was scarred from the accident, the surgeries he'd had to correct internal injuries and broken bones. But he hadn't kept that a secret, so he wouldn't stress about it. Besides, he was almost back to normal, at least when it came to sex.

After shedding his briefs, he joined her on the bed, where he removed her panties. Then they continued to kiss, to taste and caress each other until their breaths came out in jagged huffs and their hearts beat out in primal need.

When Nate knew that Anna was as ready as he was, he rolled to the side of the bed, reached into the nightstand drawer and removed a couple of condoms from the box he kept handy. He tore open one of the packages and protected them both.

He entered her slowly at first, getting the feel of her, the feel of them together. As her body responded to his, giving and taking, he increased the pace. When she cried out at the peak of her climax, he shuddered with the power of his own release and with the unspeakable pleasure they'd found in each other's arms.

Making love with Anna had been amazing. Together they…

He closed his eyes as if that might shut off the thought he'd momentarily entertained, the possibility of something more lasting than just one night, one week. One month.

"I love…" Anna paused, her thought hanging in the sex-scented air.

Nate waited for the word that would complete her

thought. Damn. She hadn't been about to say that she loved him, had she? His gut clenched, and his heart clamored with a wacky beat.

Oh, man. Don't say it, honey. Don't ruin this.

"I loved that," she said, correcting the direction her comment had nearly taken. "Making love with you…was indescribably good."

There was no question about that. It had been better than good. It had been magical. But the bigger question, his only concern, was what she'd almost said.

The word *love*, the very idea of it, set off an uneasiness that knotted up in his chest and turned his gut inside out.

Women used that word lightly. *I* love *ice cream. Don't you just* love *this dress?* But when one of them uttered it during sex, a dedicated bachelor like Nate got uneasy, even if he'd become adept at dancing around serious relationships for years.

If Anna had actually meant that she'd enjoyed their lovemaking, Nate should take pride in that. But that pause in her voice, the catch in her breath, suggested…

Oh, God. He'd known sex might throw a wrench into their otherwise well-oiled friendship, but he'd never expected her to have such an emotional response. Sure, some women did. But Anna deserved so much more than a guy like him. Hell, his very future was still so uncertain.

Nate didn't dare speak. Or breathe.

Now what?

The only answer that came to him was to cut bait, to get out of bed and to run like hell.

Anna couldn't believe she'd almost blown it. She'd known better than to say "I love you," but the words had practically jumped from her heart to her tongue. Thank goodness she'd caught herself before confessing something she wasn't quite sure she was feeling, although she suspected her gut reaction had been spot on.

Sure, whatever had swelled up in her chest during lovemaking might have been caused by sheer hormones and lust. Sex had been amazing, so maybe that was all she'd been reacting to. But right now, lying in Nate's bed, in his cozy two-story house, with baby Jessie sleeping just down the hall…

Well, it seemed that Anna's childhood dreams of having a happy home and a loving family were within reach.

She stroked Nate's upper arm, and his bicep tightened. Still, he held her close as if he wanted this moment to go on forever. She certainly did. Maybe, if he held her long enough, the change in their relationship would begin to make sense and they could consider a future of some kind together.

Moments later he pulled away to remove the condom.

"I'll be back," he said as he headed for the en-suite bathroom.

She'd be waiting for him when he returned. Then they could cuddle and talk.

A happy smile stretched across her face. Who would have thought that she'd fall for a cowboy? She certainly hadn't intended to, but sometimes the heart knew better than the mind, and all the planning in the world couldn't account for that.

Nate had no more than exited the bathroom when his cell phone rang. She assumed that he'd ignore it. Instead, he crossed the room, picked up the jeans he'd been wearing and removed the phone from the pocket.

He didn't even check the display to see who was on the other end, which struck her as a little odd. But maybe he'd been expecting a call.

"Hey," Nate said. "What's up?"

He listened a while. "Sure, I'm definitely interested. And I'd like to talk more about it."

Again, he listened. "You mean, *now*?" He shot a glance at Anna, his expression apologetic. Then he returned his focus to the caller. "Where are you?" He glanced at the clock on the bureau dresser. "It's getting late. Maybe it would be better if we met tomorrow."

Anna drew the sheet up to her chest then sat up in bed. Was he going to leave now? It was after nine o'clock. Who would request a meeting this late at night?

"I understand," Nate said. "Sure. It'll take me twenty minutes or so. And, Drew, thanks for suggesting me."

When Nate disconnected the line, he turned to Anna. A sheepish grin crossed his face. "I know this is a bad time for me to leave, but I think there's a job offer in the works. And I need to go out for about an hour. Do you mind watching the baby while I'm gone?"

"I'd be happy to. What kind of job is it? Would you be working on another ranch?"

"No, it's something else. I'd rather not say anything now and jinx it. Besides, there'd be a lot of details to work out first."

Like what? Had the intimacy they'd just shared given her the right to quiz him about it? She couldn't very well ask him not to leave and to suggest that he stay with her and…

Nate was back in the bathroom and turning on the shower before she could finish her thought. Or before she could consider what changes making love had made in their relationship.

What rights, if any, did she now have?

Maybe it was best to figure that out later. So, following Nate's lead, she got out of his bed and returned to her own room. Once inside, she closed the door. But as it clicked shut, a splash of apprehension drenched her, leaving her uneasy.

Just moments ago she'd been about to admit that she'd fallen in love with Nate. But now she was afraid of what that might mean. So where did they go from here?

At this point, the way she saw it, she only had one option. And that was to set her worries aside and to let things play out between them.

* * *

Nate's shower only lasted long enough to wash off the lingering scent of lovemaking, but he couldn't shake the guilt he felt for what he was about to do.

What kind of man left a woman in bed after a bout of lovemaking like that? Only a jerk. But when she'd said *I love...*

Okay, so she hadn't come right out and said it, but it still unnerved him. Whatever he'd started up with Anna wasn't going to be a one-night fling—and before long, before he realized what was happening, it was bound to trip him up. He had to nip it in the bud.

Something big and dark shifted inside him, opening the lid on a memory box filled with fear and dread.

Anna was the kind of woman who deserved the best a man had to offer, and Nate couldn't give her any of those things. He might have a house that was located close to the place where she worked. He also had several large bank accounts, not just his own but the one he'd inherited from Grandpa Clint. Some might think his stock portfolio was impressive.

He wouldn't have a problem sharing all of that with her, but it wasn't that easy. He also had a drawer full of belt buckles to prove that he was once a rodeo champ. Yet now he'd ended up living someone else's life. He was an imposter, and Anna needed the real deal.

All Nate had ever wanted was to be good enough so the people he cared most would be proud of him, that they'd stay in his life. Yet every one of them had abandoned him in one way or another.

Eventually, Anna would expect to have a good husband, something Nate didn't know how to be. And faking it wasn't good enough. Hell, Anna would soon see right through him. So he'd better do something to protect her before things went much further.

Damn. He glanced at his image through the fog-smudged bathroom mirror and raked a hand through his hair. He needed to get out there and talk to her, tell her all those after-the-loving things she needed to hear. But he didn't trust himself.

What if he slipped up and made promises he wouldn't be able to keep?

Nate Gallagher didn't even know how to spell *forever.*

Fortunately, Drew Madison had just given him an easy way out. Had the man called this late on any other evening, Nate might have told him a meeting with him and the rodeo promoter would have to wait until morning. But tonight?

Nate needed to escape the house before he said or did anything to regret.

Well, anything *else* he might regret.

Whatever he was feeling for Anna—and what she might be feeling for him—scared the hell out of him. It was only a matter of time before he failed the two people in this world he'd come to care for the most.

Either way, he wouldn't be a complete jerk about it. He'd talk to Anna before he left, and he'd tell her... Well, he'd tell her something, even if he wasn't sure what.

When he returned to his bedroom, she was no longer there. His conscience tweaked, making him wonder if he'd screwed up already. Either way, he only had two choices, neither of them good ones.

Still, he put on his jeans and shirt then slipped on his boots. On his way out of the house, he stopped by her room.

She'd shut the door. Did she want privacy? He stood outside for several beats, then lifted his hand and knocked softly.

She opened the door wearing a white cotton gown, something virginal and sweet. Something a new bride might wear. Her hair fell loose along her shoulders, and something warm shined in her eyes.

"When will you be back?" she asked. "Should I lock up the house for the night?"

Brighton Valley was probably the safest community in which Nate had ever lived or traveled, so he never worried about intruders. Still, he figured Anna would probably sleep more soundly if things were battened down tight for the night.

Actually, he'd feel better about leaving her and Jessie alone in the house if he made sure everything was locked up tight.

"I'm not sure how long I'll be," he said, "but don't worry. I'll make sure you're safe and sound before I go."

She nodded, obviously trusting him to do exactly what he said he'd do.

He reached out, cupping her jaw with his right hand. "I feel like a jerk for leaving you like this."

Her smile lit up, reflecting whatever lay deep in her heart. "I understand."

Did she? How could she when she had no idea what kind of crap he'd had to deal with in the past—the painful memories, the harsh lessons life had taught him?

He placed a kiss on her forehead, one that was soft and gentle. Did she realize he didn't want to hurt her, and that the only way he could do that was to leave before he got in too deep?

"Don't wait up for me," he said.

Again, her warm, trusting smile set off something wild and crazy in his chest.

"I won't," she said. "And don't worry about the baby."

As long as Anna was here, he'd never worry about Jessie.

He thanked her then turned and headed downstairs, taking the only escape route he had.

As he made his way to the driveway, where he'd parked his pickup, he realized the biggest threat to Anna and Jessie wasn't a stranger.

It was him, the man who wasn't much more than a tumbleweed rolling through their lives on the whim of a Texas breeze.

Chapter Eleven

The Stagecoach Inn was really hopping tonight, so it took Nate a while to find a parking space.

Once he'd shut off the ignition and got out of the truck, he headed for the entrance, the sound of music and laughter growing louder and more boisterous the closer he got to the door.

He hesitated a moment, his thoughts drifting to the quiet house he'd just left, to the lovely blonde he'd just made love with while soft romantic music played in the background. He had half a notion to turn around and head back home, but this was business. Rodeo promoter Ramon Esteban had a job opening according to Drew, and Nate wanted to hear what the man had to say.

Besides, it was time for a major career change.

Ever since the accident, Nate had been avoiding anyone and everything that reminded him of the rodeo. But he was just now realizing that he'd be better off working in an environment he loved, a world in which he'd once lived and thrived. So a position with Esteban Enterprises just might be the perfect job.

Up until recently, Nate would have refused to even meet with Ramon, since doing anything other than competing in an event would have been a big letdown. But then again, so was being a ranch hand on the Rocking C.

Besides, back in the day, Ramon and Grandpa Clint had been good friends, and Nate couldn't help wanting to connect with the man, even if it was only to share stories and tales of the time when Clinton McClain had been a rodeo champ.

Still, leaving Anna tonight seemed a bit like something Nate's old man might have done, but he shook off the guilt. This was different. It was business.

Nate made his way into the crowd, past the bar and the old red jukebox until he spotted both Drew and Ramon at a table in the rear of the country bar. Both men burst into broad smiles when they spotted his approach.

"Hey," Drew said, getting to his feet and extending his right hand to shake Nate's. "I'm glad you could make it. I was afraid an evening meeting on the spur of the moment wouldn't work out for you, now that you're a family man."

On the outside, maybe. Nate had a daughter, so he could understand why someone might think that.

"I've got a nanny," Nate said, perpetuating the lie he'd been living.

"That's great," Drew said. "Does she live at your house?"

"Actually, she will. I'm going to call her first thing tomorrow morning and ask her to start immediately. In the meantime, I have a sitter who's watching the baby tonight." A niggle of guilt rose up again, berating him for referring to Anna as hired help when she'd become more than that. But Nate wanted Ramon and Drew to know that having a baby wouldn't slow him down when it came to work or travel.

But wouldn't it?

"Have a seat, Nate." Ramon motioned for one of the cocktail waitresses.

"What'll you have?" she asked.

Nate had given up the hard stuff after the accident, although he was tempted to throw back a couple of tequila shooters tonight.

"Corona and lime," he said.

"You got it." The blonde turned her attention to Ramon. "Another round, fellas?"

Ramon nodded, and as the woman took off to place the orders, he leaned toward Nate. "I've got a proposition for you."

Nate studied the older man who'd been his grandpa's friend, even though thirty or more years had separated them. "I'd like to hear it."

"Henry Yeager gave his two-week notice yesterday. He's finally decided to retire and move to Arkansas, so his position at Esteban Enterprises is now open. When I mentioned that to Drew, he threw your name into the hat. And I have to say, I liked the suggestion. You've got rodeo savvy, as well as connections. I think you'd be perfect for the job. That is, if you want it."

Henry had handled a lot of the legwork for Ramon, traveling from one city to the next, setting things up for the rodeo long before opening day. And that meant Nate would be on the road and living out of a suitcase more often than not.

"I wasn't sure you'd be interested," Drew said. "What with your new family situation and all."

Nate certainly should give it a lot of thought, but he couldn't help jumping on the position before someone else caught wind of the opening and snatched it. "I'm definitely interested. And like I said, I have a dependable nanny."

"Great," Ramon said.

Was it, though? What about Jessie? He'd be on the road a lot. Of course, that's why he was hiring Barbara.

But what about Anna? Second thoughts bombarded him, throwing him into a momentary state of indecision.

Did he owe Anna anything? Better yet, did he want to feel indebted to her?

Being connected to the rodeo would give him a new identity, something he sorely needed. The traveling might get tough after a while, but that was okay. Nate wasn't the kind of guy who'd be happy in a nine-to-five job.

Again, he thought of Anna, of coming home to her each night, of sharing dinner, of going to bed together and making love as though there were no ghosts of the past and no thoughts of tomorrow.

No, that kind of life wasn't Nate's reality. He was only having weird family feelings because of the domestic routine he and Anna had fallen into lately. That's all it was.

Nate wasn't family material. Damn, look at the father he had. No, he'd been right all along. Jessie would be better off in the daily care of a good, dependable nanny.

And Anna would be happier without Nate in her life. She needed a professional man, like a doctor or lawyer. Not a damaged cowboy.

Besides, what did the two of them have in common, other than great chemistry in bed? The baby was the only thing holding him and Anna together.

Taking the job Ramon just offered him was for the best. When he told Anna what he was going to do, she'd realize that she couldn't expect more from him than he could give her, and she'd move out and get on with her own life.

And that would ensure that Nate wouldn't disappoint her in the long run.

Anna stayed up half the night, tossing and turning—and waiting for Nate to get home.

She had no idea when he finally arrived, but by the time Jessie woke up wet and hungry, Anna carried her downstairs for a bottle. Once she reached the living room, she glanced out the window and spotted his pickup in the driveway.

As if thinking Anna was dawdling, Jessie cried out.

"It's coming, sweetie." Anna shushed the baby as she headed to the kitchen then fixed the bottle.

By the time she sat down in the recliner and Jessie was nursing, Nate came downstairs. His chest was bare, and he wore only a pair of jeans, the top button undone.

"Did she give you any problems while I was gone?" he asked.

"Not a bit." On the other hand, she'd found her thoughts about Nate to be far more problematic. "How'd your meeting go?"

"Good." He ran his hand through his sleep-tousled hair, mussing it further. Oddly enough, it only made him more appealing. "In fact, it was great."

"I'm glad to hear it."

Would he go into detail? Would she have to prod him? Or, better yet, was her curiosity out of place? He'd left so soon after making love that they'd never had a chance to talk about the usual things, like, *Where do we go from here?*

After he'd left, she'd been tempted to return to his bedroom, where she could relish his scent and bask in the sweet memory of what they'd just done. But because he'd taken off so quickly, she'd felt compelled to remain in her room.

Now, as she studied him, she doubted that she'd

ever seen a sexier man. He'd obviously just rolled out of bed.

Once she was able to put the baby back in her crib, she'd like to join Nate in his room, in his bed.

"I got a job offer," Nate said. "A good one. And I'm going to take it."

He didn't look particularly thrilled, but then that might be due to the late hour, to the fact that he'd been awakened from a sound sleep.

"What would you be doing?" she asked.

"Working for Esteban Enterprises. It's an outfit that organizes and promotes rodeos."

"Congratulations." She assumed it was a local company. "Where are they based?"

"In Dallas."

She stiffened. "Will that require a move?"

"No, but it will mean I'll have to travel."

Their relationship was just getting off the ground, and while they'd never discussed what that meant…

Her thoughts stalled. He'd said he could only give her now, and not a future. But she hadn't thought he'd meant he didn't have any feelings for her.

Still, she found herself wanting to object and to ask, *What about us?* But she feared that she didn't have that right. Not yet.

Instead, she glanced down at the baby in her arms then back at Nate. "What about Jessie?"

"Barbara will be here to take care of her when I'm gone."

Anna would be around, too. But he hadn't mentioned her, hadn't suggested that she…

Actually, he hadn't said anything about the turn their relationship had taken.

But *had* it changed?

Just so there aren't any misunderstandings, he'd said prior to their lovemaking, *I can't give you all the things you need and deserve, but I can give you right now.*

She blinked back the tears filling her eyes.

"It sounds like a good opportunity for you," she said, not entirely convinced that it was.

"I agree. It's going to give me a chance to work with the rodeo again, even if I can't compete anymore."

He was more than a ranch hand. How could she fault him for wanting to do what he did best? Or rather, for wanting to work at a job he would enjoy, around people he knew and admired.

Besides, maybe his new position would only require him to leave town occasionally. "What will you do for Esteban Enterprises? How often will you need to travel?"

"I'll do all the preliminary work for the rodeos. So I'll have to spend a week or so prior to each opening day lining things up and working with the various town and city officials."

She didn't fault him for wanting that position, but how could he just pack up and leave baby Jessie with a nanny? How could he not want to parent the little girl who didn't have anyone else in the world?

And how could the man she'd come to think of as her Mr. Right just up and leave her, too?

Memories of her father, of his final walk out the door without looking back, slammed into her. And while it should have stirred up her old pain, it set off a burst of anger, too.

"But what about Jessie?" Anna asked once more.

"She'll be in good hands. If I wasn't convinced of that, I wouldn't take the job."

"But she's your daughter."

"Actually..." He paused a moment. "I'm not so sure about that."

His words nearly knocked the wind out of her. Did he honestly believe Jessie wasn't his? From what she'd heard, he'd actually hired an attorney and sought custody.

If Anna hadn't been holding the baby, she might have jumped to her feet and challenged him.

Her shocked expression must have given her away because he said, "That's not...true. Forget I said that."

How could she possibly do that? Now that it had come to light, she couldn't pretend she hadn't heard it.

"But you have custody," she said.

"Yes, I do."

Why would a man claim paternity if he didn't have good reason to believe a child was actually his?

"Are you suggesting that you might not have fathered her?"

He paled as if he wished he'd chosen his words more carefully. Then he shrugged. "Her options were limited, and I thought having me as her father would be better than nothing."

Anna's heart clenched. "How can you say that or imply you haven't bonded with her? I've seen you hold her, feed her… You *love* her."

"She's a sweet baby. And I care for her. It's just that…" He slowly shook his head. "She might be my biological daughter, but…she might not be."

"Have you had a DNA test?" she asked.

Nate shook his head. "There's no need for that. I made a commitment, and I intend to keep it. And Barbara will be able to help me. So don't worry about Jessie. She'll be fine."

At first, Anna's only concern had been about that baby, but that was no longer true. She'd gotten emotionally involved, not just with Jessie, but with Nate. And now he was threatening to leave, without giving a single thought to what they might have had.

After all the time and effort she put into him, into…*them*, he was going to dash her hopes and dreams.

"We made love," she said. "Didn't that mean anything to you?"

"Yes, it meant a lot. But I'll never be able to give you the things you need, the things you deserve."

Her father had said something similar before he moved on with his life. But when he'd left, his words to her mother had been laced with anger and resentment. On the other hand, Nate's had been soft and sure. Still, they cut Anna just as deeply, ripping a jagged tear in her heart.

It crushed her to think of what might have been, if Nate had been the man she'd once thought he was, and her ego took a hard blow. She wanted to lash out, to strike out and hurt him, just as he'd hurt her.

"I have needs, all right, but you have no idea what they are. And I'd never expect you to fulfill them." Anna set the bottle on the lamp table and slowly got to her feet so she wouldn't wake the sleeping baby. "But Jessie has needs, too. And you made a commitment to see to every last one of them when you signed those custody papers."

"I'm committed to her—at least, the best way I know how to be."

Who was this man? Just hours ago, Anna had hoped—no, she'd just *assumed*—that he would step up to be the husband and daddy she'd always dreamed of having in her life. Instead, Nate had fallen into the same irresponsible behavior as her father had when he packed his bags and left her and her mother for good.

Anna took one last glance at Jessie then handed the precious bundle to Nate. "Here, you take her. I'm going to pack my stuff and leave."

"It's three in the morning," he said, taking his daughter. "Where do you think you're going?"

"Back to the Night Owl Motel."

Nate clicked his tongue. "You can't go there at this hour."

"Sure I can. And if they don't have a room available for me, I'll sleep in my car."

"That's not a wise idea."

She stiffened, her hackles rising with each tick of the clock on the mantel. "Let's not talk about making well-thought-out decisions, shall we?"

What appeared to be concern was splashed across Nate's face. "If you're going to insist on leaving, would you please wait until daylight?"

He had a point, but she was too angry to admit it. Still, she couldn't very well drive off in a huff. What if the No Vacancy sign was lit? What would she do then? Where would she go?

She'd better give them a call first because she really wasn't about to sleep in her car at a truck stop.

The baby, who was the reason Anna was here in the first place, squirmed in Nate's arms as if she'd heard the heated discussion and was uneasy about her future. As she well should be.

Anna might want to walk out on Nate and never speak to him again, but she wouldn't abandon Jessie. That child needed a loving parent. And if Nate wasn't going to do right by her, then Anna would.

For the second time since she'd had to call in Protective Services to remove Danny Walker from his home, she felt like a failure. How had she missed seeing the signs with Nate?

God, maybe she'd made the wrong career choice.

Either way, she wasn't about to turn her back on Jessie, whom she'd come to love. This was personal now.

Could Anna adopt her as a single mother?

First thing in the morning, she'd seek out her options. But for now, she was going to leave the room before she said or did anything she might regret.

Like break down and cry in front of the man who'd stomped on her heart and dashed her fragile dream of finally having a real family of her own.

Last night, after putting Jessie back in her crib, Nate hadn't slept a wink. Instead, he'd listened to the sound of the breeze on the windows and the house creaking in complaint.

He hated the idea of being at odds with Anna, but it was better to have it happen now than after they got involved any deeper. At least, that's what he kept telling himself.

Finally, just before sunrise, he rolled out of bed and headed to the kitchen for some strong morning java, robust and laden with caffeine.

When he reached Anna's bedroom, the door was wide open, the bed made. Something deep in his chest clenched, and a blast of heavy emotion threatened to consume him.

Had she left anyway? For good?

He ought to be happy that he'd freed himself of a relationship that would only lead to his failure and to her heartbreak. But he wasn't.

If he'd done the right thing, then why did his chest ache as if she'd broken something inside?

He blew out a sigh then went downstairs. While he

waited for the coffee to brew, he placed a couple of phone calls. The first was to Sam, letting him know he'd be late to work.

Sam told him not to worry about it, and Nate let it go at that. He would have to tell Sam that he'd give him two weeks as an acting foreman. After that, Sam would have to find someone else or cut his honeymoon short. But that was a discussion Nate wanted to have in person.

Next he placed the call to Barbara Newcomb, only to realize he'd awoken the poor woman from a sound sleep.

"I'm sorry, Barbara. I didn't realize it was so early."

"No problem. I had a late night chatting with a friend from high school. What can I do for you?"

"I called to offer you the nanny position, if you'd like it."

"That's wonderful news. When would you like me to start?"

Nate glanced at the clock on the microwave, realizing what he was going to suggest might be impossible. "As soon as you can get here." Then he managed a little chuckle, letting her know that he wouldn't expect that quick of a response.

"I'm afraid I can't start today. I have plans for the rest of the week. My friend and I are going to drive down to Galveston and spend a few days at a B and B. Would it be all right if I started on Monday morning? I could arrive the night before."

If that was the only option. He'd also have to ask

Joy and the nurses to help him out until then. "That'll be fine, Barbara. I'll see you Sunday evening."

After downing a cup of coffee, Nate went upstairs to the nursery and packed the diaper bag. Then he carefully removed Jessie from the crib without waking her, placed her in the car seat and left the house.

He used to dread the forty-minute drive to the ranch, but today he was looking forward to putting some distance between him and the two-story house that had almost begun to feel like a real home.

Once he arrived at the ranch, and before he shut off the ignition, he spotted Sam and Joy standing on the wraparound porch. The attractive older woman had just handed the foreman a white mug, and they were both smiling, their love and happiness hard to ignore.

Grandpa Clint and Audrey had cared for each other and had what appeared to be a good marriage, but Nate hadn't ever seen them gaze at each other the way Joy and Sam did. Those two had something special.

Thoughts of Anna came to mind. What would their relationship have become, if he hadn't ended it before it had a chance to develop?

He shook his head, letting the image drift away, refusing to dwell on what wasn't meant to be, and got out of the pickup. Then he grabbed the diaper bag and removed the carrier from the backseat. He made his way to the porch just as Jessie began to squint her eyes and squirm.

"I hope you don't mind," Nate told Sam and Joy. "I'm going to need a sitter today and for the rest of the week. But don't worry. I've hired a nanny who'll start on Monday."

"Are you kidding?" Joy beamed. "We've missed that sweet baby. Take her inside. I'll be there shortly. I just need to work out a couple of wedding details."

Nate had no more than turned to the door when Joy added, "Pour yourself a cup of coffee. I just made a fresh pot. And there's still some ham and scrambled eggs on the stove."

"Thanks." Nate had hardly made it through the living room when he was met by Alicia, one of the RNs who worked at the ranch.

"Well, look who's here!" Alicia broke into a warm smile. "We were afraid you wouldn't bring Jessie back to see us."

"I hope you don't mind watching her for the next couple of days."

"Are you kidding? We'd love to."

When Jessie began to fuss, Alicia added, "Give her to me. I'll feed her."

"Thanks. I'd appreciate that." Nate crossed the room and entered the kitchen, where one of his favorite old cowboys sat at the table, enjoying a cup of coffee.

"Look who decided to have breakfast with us again," Rex Mayberry said. "I thought you'd fallen head over heels for that pretty social worker and run off to marry her."

"No chance of that." Nate wasn't sure what he'd

been feeling for Anna, but marriage had always been out of the question.

"So no wedding bells for you?" Rex asked.

"I'm afraid not. Some men just aren't the marrying kind." Others sabotaged a good thing before it could blow up in their faces.

"Too bad," Rex said. "A little romance never hurt anyone."

Nate could have argued that point. Whatever romance he'd had with Anna had stirred up plenty of hurt in him.

Rex got up from the table and went to the sink, where he poured out the rest of his coffee. Then he glanced out the window and into the yard, where Joy and Sam now stood. "They got something special, don't they?"

It sure seemed that way.

"Me and my wife had something special, too," Rex added, "although we nearly split up a couple of times, mostly because of my stubbornness. But bless her heart, she stuck it out, and we shared twenty-seven more good years together. She's gone now, and I'd give anything to have her back."

"I guess there aren't too many relationships like that."

Rex chuffed. "More than some might think."

Again Nate wanted to argue, but what did he know about love and lifetime commitments?

Under normal circumstances, he would have steered the conversation into a completely different and much safer direction. But for some reason he said, “I don't remember my parents ever being happy. The closest thing to a real marriage I ever witnessed was the one my grandfather and Audrey had. And their relationship didn't appear to be all that special to me.”

“I know what you mean,” Rex said. “I'm sure they were fairly happy, but not like they should have been.”

Nate studied the old man, wondering just how much he knew about the couple—probably a lot more than Nate did.

“Did you know that Audrey and your grandpa used to be high school sweethearts?” Rex asked.

That was news to Nate. They'd gotten married late in life, so he'd just assumed they hadn't known each other when they were younger. “Why didn't they get married back then?”

“I'm sure that had been Audrey's plan, but then Clint met a redhead with a penchant for rodeo cowboys and parties. She got pregnant, so Clint married her.”

“Was that my grandmother?” Nate asked.

“I 'spect it was. Clint only had one kid, a daughter he adored. That's why he stayed with his wife—until she ran off with a slick-talking car salesman, taking your mama with her. It dang near broke Clint's heart, especially when she moved on without a forwarding address.”

Nate hadn't realized that. If he had, it would have given him one more reason not to risk love or marriage.

"Your grandfather remained single and committed to his career for a long time. And Audrey got married along the way, but the guy up and died on her. She'd been widowed for years when she and Clint hooked up again."

"That's nice," Nate said. "I'm glad they found each other and didn't have to spend their last years alone."

"I hear you." Rex slowly shook his gray head.

"My grandfather never mentioned his first wife—or even my mother," Nate said.

"That's probably because he didn't have the chance to know your mom. She was just a toddler when your grandma ran off with her."

"I wish he would have said something."

"Maybe he just didn't want to make Audrey uncomfortable. She might have resented the fact that if things had been different, she might have had kids and a family of her own."

"Maybe that's why she never quite warmed to me," Nate said.

"If she didn't, that was her loss. Some people refuse to break free from the chains of the past. But the smart ones will." Rex sat back in his chair, folded his arms across his chest and smirked. "But I gotta tell you, son. You can blame your family or fate or whatever situation might have brought you to your knees, but there will come a day when you finally realize that life is too damn short to be thick-skinned and mule-headed."

As usual, Rex had a reason for his story, a lesson to teach. And it gave Nate pause.

He'd had a lot of bad breaks over the years. He'd lost his mom as a kid and had been left with an alcoholic father. He'd been sent to foster care as a teenager. And he'd suffered a career-ending accident when Fire in the Hole trampled him.

But Rex had a point. If Nate wanted to be thick-skinned and mule-headed, he could blame fate or his old man for the rest of his life. But he had to take ownership of his life now.

So where did he go from here?

Chapter Twelve

Nate worked his tail off all day, hoping the physical labor would keep his mind off his troubles. But no matter what he did, his worries continued to haunt him until Sam stepped off the wraparound porch and called him into the ranch house for dinner.

Normally, Nate had a big appetite, especially when it came to eating whatever Joy had prepared for the oldsters and the hands, but there was too much going on in his brain to even think about food.

Besides, he needed to have that chat with Sam, and now seemed like as good a time as ever.

"Can we talk for a minute?" Nate asked the foreman. *"Alone?"*

"Sure." Sam crossed the lawn and met Nate in the yard.

"I need some fatherly advice, and since my grandpa's gone, I figure you're the next best thing."

"I'll take that as a compliment, son."

Nate's only response was a nod. "I really appreciate this job, Sam. And I plan to help you out while you're on your honeymoon, but..."

"But it's time for you to move on." Sam removed his hat and wiped his brow with the sleeve of his red flannel shirt. "I knew working here was just a temporary fix to your troubles. And I know we haven't been able to pay you what you're worth."

"It was never about money," Nate said.

"I know that, too. Your grandpa and I were pretty tight, and I have a pretty good idea how much he made with the sale of the Double M. So my guess is that you've got plenty of cash in reserve. Enough to even buy your own ranch, if you wanted to."

Nate knew Sam wasn't poking for details. He was just making a good assumption. "You're right. I've got enough to buy a respectable spread, but that ranch would never be the Double M."

"I know." Sam placed a hand on Nate's shoulder, his grip sure and steady. "And I suspect the fact that Clint sold it without telling you probably still eats at you. But your grandfather had his reasons for selling it so quickly. Audrey was diagnosed with cancer, and he wanted to make sure they could spend some quality time together before she passed."

"Audrey was *dying*?" Nate tried to reel in his surprise, but it was pretty hard to do after the fact.

"She'd been in and out of remission for years, but

the most recent bout of chemo didn't do the trick. Clint didn't know how much time she had left. He wanted her to have an experimental treatment and wasn't sure what it might end up costing."

Grandpa Clint had obviously shared all of that with Sam. Why hadn't he told Nate?

Damn, how long had she been sick? Was that why she'd seemed to keep her distance? Were there days when she'd been too ill to come out of her room?

"My grandpa never said a thing to me," Nate said. "I guess that just goes to show you we weren't all that close."

"I suggested he level with you, but he figured you'd been through too much already. And he was hoping she'd get better."

Shocked and speechless, Nate blew out a ragged sigh.

"Ironic," Sam said. "Isn't it? Clint knew he'd be losing his wife in the upcoming months. He just hadn't expected to go out with her in a car accident."

Nate had no idea what to say, what to think.

"You'd been through so much, first with your own accident, then with Clint's death. So when I heard you were ready to go back to work, I figured the Rocking C would be the perfect place for you to start."

"Working here has been good for me," Nate admitted. "But just so you know, I've been offered a position with Esteban Enterprises."

"How do you feel about that?"

"Truthfully? I'm both excited and torn. That position would require me to travel. A lot."

"And now you have a baby to think about," Sam said, "a family to consider."

"That's about the size of it. I want to be a good father, but I never had a good role model."

"You had Clint."

"Yes, and he taught me how to be a good man, a good cowboy. But as you've probably already figured out, we didn't share too many personal thoughts or feelings."

"Sometimes it's easier to clam up," Sam said. "But as you've seen, that's not always the case."

"What do I know about being a family man?" Nate asked.

"I suspect you have a pretty good idea about what *not* to be."

Sam had that right.

"When I was a kid," Nate admitted, "I remember running up to my old man for a hug or reassurance or whatever. And most of the time, he'd push me away. After a while, you stop expecting any affection."

"The way I see it," Sam said, "you've done some pushing away yourself."

The words, the truth, slammed into Nate with a brutal wallop. But then, how in the world would Sam know about Anna, about what Nate had done to keep her from getting too close?

"Last I heard," Sam said, "that pretty social worker was staying with you and looking after Jessie. But looks like you lost her—as a sitter, a roommate or… whatever."

Nate had lost her all right. But only because he'd

pushed her away. “Hell, Sam. Anna’s better off without me. I’m too messed up.”

Sam slowly shook his head. “That’s not true. And don’t you believe it. You’re a fine, upstanding man—and a damn good cowboy, whether you’re competing in the rodeo or working with horses on a ranch. Granted, you might have messed up with Anna. And if that was the case, you’ll just need to make things right.”

Sam undoubtedly had a point, but Nate had no idea where to start.

Anna had no more than checked into her new room at the Night Owl Motel, set out her toiletries in the bathroom and hung her clothes up in the small closet when her cell phone rang.

Carla, her landlord, told her the work had finally been completed on the studio apartment, and she could return whenever she wanted to.

How was that for luck?

If that call had come in just fifteen minutes earlier, she’d be able to drive straight home. But now?

She would have to present her case to the clerk at the front desk and hope to get a refund. So she packed up her belongings. She’d just reached for her suitcase handle when a knock sounded at the motel room door. She let out a huff and went to see who it was. The maid, she assumed. But when she spotted Nate standing in the doorway, his hat in hand, her jaw dropped and it took her a moment to recover.

"What do you want?" she asked—and not very nicely.

"I came because I owe you an apology. And I think we need to have a heart-to-heart talk."

She wanted to slam the door in his face, but that wouldn't do her any good. Not if there was a chance he might release custody of the baby to her. So she stepped aside and let him into the small room.

He glanced at the bed, where her packed suitcase rested. "I take it you just arrived."

"Yes, but I'm going to check out. I just learned that my place is finally ready, so I'm going home."

"Then I'm glad I caught you before you left."

Anna folded her arms across her chest. She might not want to stir up anything with a man who could become a legal adversary, but she didn't have to make things easy for him. "So what was it you wanted to say?"

"First of all, I was a jerk and said a lot of things I didn't mean. You have no idea how sorry I am. You didn't deserve to be treated that way, especially after…what we shared."

As much as she'd like to hold on to her anger and hurt feelings, it wouldn't do her or the baby any good. "Apology accepted."

Nate glanced down at his boots, and when he looked up, she spotted something raw and vulnerable in his eyes, something that told her this wasn't easy for him.

"That accident damn near killed me," he said. "And I'm not just talking about the broken bones and internal injuries. It stole my very identity. At least, that's what I thought for the longest time."

"I'm sorry that your life didn't turn out the way you wanted it to. But that doesn't mean you don't have value or other options."

"I realize that now. The job at the Rocking C was just something to keep me busy while I figured out what I wanted to do. And now I have a pretty good idea."

"You want to remain involved with the rodeo," she said. "Believe it or not, I get that. But Jessie deserves to have a full-time parent. And I'd be more than happy to take custody—if you'll sign it over."

He paled, and his lips parted. It seemed to take him a moment to recover. "Are you suggesting that I give Jessie up? To *you*?"

That was exactly what she was getting at, although she hadn't meant to blindside him. But the whole idea had taken her a little by surprise, too. "I didn't expect it to happen, but I love that little girl. And I want to do whatever I can to ensure she's raised in a happy, loving home."

"I can't do that," he said. "She's… I'm…"

"You wouldn't give her up, even if it turns out that she's not your biological daughter?"

He studied her for the longest moment then slowly shook his head. "No, I wouldn't do that. I've been doing a lot of thinking. And I've come to a couple of conclusions I should have realized a long time ago."

"What's that?"

"The reason I refused to be tested earlier—at least, the reason I latched on to—was that I was afraid that she might not be my daughter. Kenny Huddleston, the man who beat Jessie's mom to death, was married to her. So there's a possibility he's her father. He might be serving time in jail for what he did, but what if one of his family members were to step up and want her?"

Anna hadn't realized Nate had been trying to protect Jessie. "But if she *is* a Huddleston, and if someone—an aunt or uncle, a grandparent—wants to raise her—"

"No!" Nate shook his head. "I can't let that happen. You don't know those people. Kenny has some shady relatives, several of whom have been arrested and convicted of crimes like assault, drunk and disorderly conduct or driving while under the influence."

Anna hadn't realized any of that. No wonder Nate was so adamant about retaining custody. It also meant she couldn't challenge his paternity or his ability to parent. She couldn't risk doing anything that would give that precious baby to anyone who'd mistreat her or lead her astray. "I'm sorry, Nate. I had no idea you had gone so far to protect Jessie."

He chuffed then shook his head again. "But do you know what's even scarier to me? It's learning that she actually is my daughter. As long as I was doing a good deed, like taking in a little one with no place better to be, I really couldn't fail her. But if I am her father, then she's stuck with me."

As angry as Anna had been, as hurt by Nate's complete disregard of her feelings, sympathy rose up in their place, chasing the bitterness away. Nate was an amazing man, flawed a bit, but full of love and kindness. He wanted to be a good father, but was afraid he didn't know how. Without a thought, she reached out and stroked his upper arm. "Ever since moving into your house, I've watched the two of you. I've seen you feed her and cuddle her. You've been giving Jessie exactly what she needs."

"Thank you for that. It helps to know you have faith in me. And while we're on the touchy-feely stuff—and my struggle to deal with emotions, mine or anyone else's—Jessie wasn't the only one who scared the living hell out of me." Nate reached for Anna's hand and gave it a gentle squeeze. "You've got me squirming inside, too, honey."

Her heart fluttered, ready to take flight. "How so?"

"In the past, I chose to walk away from people who got too close and who might expect more from a relationship than I was able or willing to give. But that's about to change."

Did she dare ask him to explain?

"I'm going to have that DNA test, although the results won't matter. I'm already in love with that baby girl."

"I'm glad to hear it." But Anna wasn't quite ready to walk away from Jessie's life. Or to turn her back on Nate. If he'd give her any reason to think or hope—

"But that's not all. I'm also in love with *you*. And the thought of losing either one of you, let alone both, scares me more than instant fatherhood once did."

Anna could scarcely believe what he was saying. "You love *me*?"

"I probably should apologize to you for that." Nate shook his head. "Damn, I can't believe I said that."

"I heard it with my own ears, so don't try to back-pedal on me now. Are you sure about this? About *us*?"

A grin stretched across his face. "I'm as sure as a broken-down cowboy can be."

"You may have been hurt and knocked down more times than was fair, but you're not the least bit damaged, Nate."

"When it comes to the ideal man for you, I'm going to probably fall short more times than not. I knew that all along, so just thinking that you might love me, at least a little, made me want to run for the hills."

She smiled. "Or straight to the rodeo?"

He lifted her hand to his lips and brushed a kiss on her knuckles. "At that time I wanted to get as far away from you as possible. But I've been running from people and feelings for way too long. And I'm tired of avoiding the things I need most in my life. And that's love and a family."

"I can't believe this," she said.

"Oh, you can believe it."

She laughed and scanned the small, outdated motel room then looked back at Nate. "Over the years I had a lot of ideas of what the setting would be like when I first told a man that I loved him. I could envision a walk on the beach or even a balcony like Juliet's. But I never expected to be in a cheap motel room."

"Oh, I plan to repeat this scene over and over again. We'll take that walk, and I'll find the perfect balcony."

"I just might hold you to it."

"And now that I got up the nerve to lay my heart on the line," Nate said, drawing her into his arms. "I'm going all the way with this."

She wasn't sure what he meant, and her head tilted slightly to the side.

"I'm a far cry from perfect, Anna, but if you'll have me, I promise to be the best husband and father I can be."

"You're close enough to perfect for me." Then she slipped her hands around his neck and kissed him with all the love in her heart.

One week later, on a sunny afternoon, Nate and Anna attended Sam and Joy's wedding at the Rocking Chair Ranch, along with a small but happy gathering of retired cowboys, ranch hands, nurses and various friends within the community.

They'd left Jessie at home with the new nanny, who was working out like a charm. Barbara was not only competent, but loving, too. In fact, two days after she moved in, Anna had gone back to work at the medical center, confident the baby was well cared for.

Now, as they sat outside in rows of white chairs brought in by a party rental company, a slight breeze stirred up the scent of hay and the hearty spread of food being placed on long tables by the catering staff. A rented white gazebo had been brought in and adorned with flowers. There the bride and groom would say their vows.

The pastor of the community church stood at the ready, his Bible open, while Sam and his nephew Blake Darnell waited for Joy to come down the makeshift aisle.

One of the oldsters sat in a chair near the gazebo, playing a guitar. As the chords shifted, signaling the start of the short bridal procession, the pastor indicated that the audience should stand.

Nate reached for Anna's hand, giving it a gentle squeeze. They'd already begun talking about their own wedding plans. It was interesting. Nate had held back his feelings for so long that she'd feared it would be a struggle for him to share his thoughts and emotions. But once he'd opened up, it seemed to be easier for him with each passing day.

True to his word, he'd requested a paternity test. And just yesterday, they'd gotten the results. Nate Gallagher was Jessica's biological daddy. And soon, Anna would be her mommy.

Shannon Cramer Darnell, Blake's new wife and Joy's niece, started down the aisle wearing a soft yellow gown and carrying a bouquet of spring flowers. Before marrying Blake, the lovely brunette had once been the head nurse at the Rocking Chair Ranch. And now she was in medical school in California.

Again the guitar chords changed, and Joy started down the aisle. The redhead might be in her late sixties, but Anna didn't think she'd ever seen a more beautiful bride—certainly not one who was happier.

"Dearly beloved," the pastor said, drawing the attention of all who were seated in the white fold-up chairs on the lawn. "We are gathered together..."

What a happy day. And not just for the newlyweds.

After Joy and Sam returned from their honeymoon, Nate would go to work for Esteban Enterprises. His new boss had agreed to let him stay on at the Rocking C until Sam returned to take over again himself. He'd also promised to find another position in the company that wouldn't require as much travel.

In the meantime, Anna and Nate would plan their own wedding—and begin their lives as husband and wife, daddy and mommy.

Nate might not be the groom she'd had in mind when she'd imagined getting married one day, but she didn't want another man. He'd proven to her that the image she'd once had of Mr. Right no longer existed.

Nate was a keeper, flaws and all.

When the vows had been said, and Sam and Joy were officially married, the audience erupted in cheers. Well, make that yee-haws and hoots.

As she and Nate made their way to the rented tables that had been set up for the reception, Anna said, "What do you think? Is this the kind of wedding you'd like?"

"I'm happy with whatever you want. All I know is that I want to go to bed with you each night and wake up with you in my arms. I want to create a family—for all of us. And for any other kids we might have."

"I'm good with that," Anna said. Then she wrapped her arms around the man she loved and kissed him.

They would create a family together—one that would undoubtedly be flawed. Yet she had no doubt that it would be perfect in all the ways that mattered.

* * * * *

Look for Drew and Lainie's story,
the next installment in
ROCKING CHAIR RODEO,
the new series by
USA TODAY *bestselling author Judy Duarte.*
Coming soon to Mills & Boon Cherish!

And don't miss Blake and Shannon's story,
ROPING IN THE COWGIRL,
available wherever Mills & Boon books
and ebooks are sold!

MILLS & BOON®

EXCLUSIVE EXTRACT

Miranda Marlowe has just discovered
she's pregnant with her boss's baby...

Read on for a sneak preview of
HER PREGNANCY BOMBSHELL

Tomorrow she would go down to the beach, feel the sand beneath her feet, let the cold water of the Mediterranean run over her toes. Then, like an old lady, she would go and lie up to her neck in a rock pool heated by the hot spring and let its warmth melt away the confused mix of feelings; the desperate hope that she would turn around, Cleve would be there and, somehow, everything would be back to normal.

It wasn't going to happen and she wasn't going to burden Cleve with this.

She'd known what she was doing when she'd chosen to see him through a crisis in the only way she knew how.

She'd seen him at his weakest, broken, weeping for all that he'd lost, and she'd left before he woke so that he wouldn't have to face her. Struggle to find something to talk about over breakfast.

She'd known that there was only ever going to be one end to the night they'd spent together. One of them would have to walk away and it couldn't be Cleve.

Four weeks ago she was an experienced pilot working

for Goldfinch Air Services, a rapidly expanding air charter and freight company. She could have called any number of contacts and walked into another job.

Three weeks and six days ago she'd spent a night with the boss and she was about to become a cliché. Pregnant, single and grounded.

She'd told the border official that she was running away and she was, but not from a future in which there would be two of them. The baby she was carrying was a gift. She was running away from telling Cleve that she was pregnant.

She needed to sort out exactly what she was going to do before, have a plan firmly in place, everything settled, so that when she told him the news he understood that she expected nothing. That he need do nothing...